To Aaron

BAD TO
THE LAST
DROP

Enjoy to
The last drop!
Deb Lewis

Pat Ondarko

BAD TO THE LAST DROP

DEB LEWIS &
PAT ONDARKO

LANGDON STREET PRESS
MINNEAPOLIS

Langdon Street Press
212 3rd Avenue North, Suite 290
Minneapolis, MN 55401
612.455.2293
www.langdonstreetpress.com

ISBN - 978-1-934938-56-0
ISBN - 1-934938-56-4
LCCN - 2009932399

Book sales for North America and international:
Itasca Books, 3501 Highway 100 South, Suite 220
Minneapolis, MN 55416
Phone: 952.345.4488 (toll free 1.800.901.3480)
Fax: 952.920.0541; email to orders@itascabooks.com

Cover Design & typeset by Kristeen Wegner.

Printed in the United States of America

LANGDON
STREET PRESS

Dedicated to the people who walk in the shadows of life

and to all those who go to war and return home

in a broken state.

PROLOGUE

IT WAS WELL AFTER ONE O'CLOCK WHEN IT WAS FINALLY FINISHED. I COULDN'T STOP A smug, self-satisfied smirk from moving across my face as I glanced about the apartment. Cups and plates were neatly stacked back in the cupboard. The table was wiped clean, and the floor was swept. Even the old scraggly broom was placed in the corner.

"Just right," I whispered. The soft words seemed to echo through the rooms, as if the walls themselves already knew.

Irritation suddenly tightened my chest, as I noticed how threadbare everything around me was — the faded curtains; the stains on the carpet. Even the dishes I had so carefully cleaned were chipped. *All that money going to waste.*

And then I giggled. *Well, not* all *of it.*

I reached for the knob on the old wooden door, and as I did, I glanced at the room one final time. My eyes flitted from place to place like a small bird, quick and inquisitive, until my gaze finally came to rest on the overstuffed chair, placed in a prominent spot in the room.

"Should I leave the light on? The TV, perhaps?" I inquired brightly. The figure in the chair seemed almost molded into it. "No? I suppose not."

The room was quiet, as a room can get only in winter. Funny how little difference the quiet made. One moment, he had been sitting there raging at me, and the next …

Now, with hands on hips, I pretended to pout. "Really, you shouldn't have threatened me. It's your own fault, you know." Turning once again to the door, I grabbed the knob in my gloved hand, eager to be gone. I flipped off the light switch and quietly closed the door behind me, the lock making a small click as it moved into place.

What a beautiful winter night, I thought. Whistling *It's Beginning to Look a Lot Like Christmas*, I made my way home.

Chapter One

ON A CLEAR, SUNNY SEPTEMBER MORNING, DEB LINBERG PULLED HER WHITE PRIUS into a parking space in front of the Black Cat Coffeehouse. Standing near the front door was Joe, one of the town regulars who frequented the Black Cat—Joe had all but worn a constant path between the Black Cat and his small apartment across the street. Tall and stocky, he was most recognizable by his black eye patch and a lit cigarette dangling from the side of his mouth. Deb noticed Joe conversing with Jack Swanson, the mayor of Ashland. As she got out of the car, Deb wondered what scheme Joe would tell her about this time. As soon as he saw her, Joe turned from the mayor and smiled broadly.

"Hey, Deb, how are you doing? It's a great day! Want to know why?" Without waiting for an answer, Joe continued all at once, hardly stopping to catch his breath between sentences. "Because I'm definitely going to win the lottery today! No doubt about it. And when I do, I'm kissing this place good-bye forever. I'm out of here! I'll be moving to Florida with five beautiful Russian women, and we'll be spending our time on a boat, loaded with nothing but brandy! And you won't be seeing me any more!"

"Hey, that sounds really great, Joe," Deb replied politely, more than a little bemused. Though many people seemed frightened or intimidated by Joe's overt friendliness and his odd appearance, Deb never had that concern; Joe simply appeared to have an insatiable desire for human contact. Joe opened the door to the coffeehouse and followed Deb as she stood in line to order coffee.

1

So he's on his lottery kick today, Deb thought.

"Guess what I did yesterday?" Joe asked without preamble.

Here it comes, she thought. *I know where this is going.* Still, she played along, even though she was slightly irritated. "I don't know. What did you do yesterday?"

"I called the CIA to tell them what I thought about their eavesdropping. It took me at least ten tries to get through, and then the SOBs didn't even want to talk to me!" Joe replied; his voice was loud enough for everyone at the Black Cat to hear.

The few patrons seated in the big front room pointedly turned to their newspapers or their private conversations. Deb, as usual, tried to listen politely. Sometimes, Deb tried to encourage Joe out of his paranoia—there were times when Joe was lucid and that made for interesting conversation—but today was not a day when Deb had the energy to try to engage with him. Today, her response (or lack of one) didn't seem to matter to Joe.

Turning from Deb, Joe smiled at an elderly gentleman in line behind him and repeated the same fantasy about winning the lottery. The man ignored Joe and blew past him without acknowledging his presence.

Poor Joe, Deb thought. *His time in 'Nam really messed him up.* She walked out into the sunlight, leaving Joe to work the room like a politician.

Chapter Two

PAT KERRY PUT HER FEET UP ON A CHAIR AND GAVE A HAPPY SIGH AS THE FIRST SIP OF hot Italian roast warmed her right down to her toes. It had been a frosty autumn walk to the coffeehouse in this northern Wisconsin town—one of many walks since her recent move here—but it was worth it. *A little exercise never hurt anyone*, Pat thought. *Emphasis on "little."* She looked across the table at her best friend, Deb Linberg.

"Well, I just felt we should *do* something," Deb said as she read the *Daily Press*. "So I wrote a letter to the editor about Joe."

"Good idea," Pat responded. Smiling, she took another sip of her coffee, avoiding Deb's eyes. *Good old Deb*, Pat thought. *A woman of action*.

"What are you smiling at?" Deb asked, looking up over her glasses. "Are you laughing at me?"

"No ... well ... maybe a little," Pat conceded. "I was just thinking that when we're ninety-two years old, we'll still be sitting in the Black Cat, drinking coffee, and deciding what our latest cause will be."

"For your information, Joe is *not* a cause," Deb retorted focusing on the paper once more. "He's dead; he can't *be* a cause. I just think someone should remember him."
She sighed. "No one should just die and not be missed for four whole days—and then to be found by the kid who works the coffee counter, for goodness sake!"

Just a few days earlier, Sam, the barista, had wiped the long wooden counter during a brief reprieve from his early-morning rush hour of regulars. As he caught his breath, Sam noticed that Joe had not yet made his customary appearance. *Strange,* Sam mused. *Joe wasn't here yesterday or the day before that, either. Come to think of it, it must be at least three days since I last saw him in here.*

Sam tried to recall any conversations he'd overheard that made mention of a trip. Usually, Joe talked endlessly and loudly whenever he made plans to go anywhere. Every customer who would listen was informed—in great detail—of any changes to Joe's usual restless routine of pacing back and forth and in and out of the coffee shop. Joe was a predictable fixture in the place, as much a part of the scene as the aroma of good coffee and the art on the walls displayed by local artists. The Black Cat Coffeehouse was one of those small-town places where the regulars were like an odd family, where everyone—but especially Sam—looked out for each other.

Something just doesn't seem right, Sam thought. *If Joe doesn't show up by the end of my shift, I'll call someone. Let's see ... what did Joe tell me about his family? Something about a brother and two sisters. The brother was local ... Jake, or something like that. No ... Jacob. I'll see if I can find a number in the book when I get a minute.*

He looked up with a smile as a biker came through the door. "Can I help you?" Sam asked.

Later that afternoon, with still no sign of Joe, Sam started digging for Joe's brother's phone number. After several tries, he finally reached Joe's brother, Jacob Abramov in Hurley, who said he had not heard from Joe for a week. "That's not all that unusual," Jacob had said, "since Joe only calls every few weeks anyway."

Sam sensed a lack of support from Jacob, so without mentioning his reason for calling, he simply said, "Thanks. Good-bye." Then he hung up and made a decision to call the police.

They'll think I'm crazy if this turns out to be nothing more than Joe acting impulsively and taking a quick trip south without telling anyone. Still, this is a small town, after all, and a place where people still look out for each other.

Brushing aside his nagging doubts, Sam dialed the Ashland Police Department non-emergency number.

Pat took another sip of coffee, enjoying the idea of being able to sit as long as she liked—every day, if she liked—even more than the taste of the strong brew. Idly, she wondered if anyone would offer to do a memorial service for the indigent man or if maybe she should. *Nope,* she told herself, sternly, *I've taken a year off from ministry in the Lutheran church for a reason, and I refuse to get pulled back into it all, even if it's for a good cause. No exceptions. Do one funeral, then someone else will find out and pretty soon I'll be doing weddings in the park and funerals for people without a church affiliation, and then someone's aunt will need a cheerful visit at the hospital.* She reached for her bagel. *Nope, I will not bring it up.* She put an extra dab of cream cheese on for good measure and took a big bite—after all, she had walked all the way from her house—and then took the paper from Deb's outstretched hand.

"Funny," Deb said, as she put down the paper, "that he died *now*, isn't it? He was only fifty-seven, the paper says, and even though he was a character, he didn't look sick or anything."

"I'm sure they'll do an autopsy, but he *was* a crazy, all his talk about calling the CIA and the army," Pat countered. "Who knows what meds he was taking or what he was mixing it with? You know how he talked about drinking brandy. I have to admit, I will miss his coming in here every day, stopping at every table, talking to everyone. Truth is, if you wrote about a character like him in the mysteries I read, with his eye patch and crazy talk, it would be unbelievable."

"Judging the book by his cover again, Pat? Besides, even paranoids are sane part of the time."

"But you have to admit he is—was—an interesting character. All his stories about what he'd do when he won the lottery—he was going to buy an island. And bring five—what was it?—oh, right, five Russian women to live with him and drink brandy all night long. You know, I'm sorry I never asked him why five? I mean, why not three ... or ten? And he didn't just come in the Black Cat. He walked all over town, going in the bank and the stores, doing the same thing. He thought there were conspiracy plots everywhere. The school board was stealing the education money. Someone at the bank was changing the amount in his account." Pat shook her head as she glanced briefly around the brightly lit room of gathered coffee drinkers. "But you're right, he wasn't crazy all the time, just a few days before he ... well, he got to talking about Shakespeare, and I really couldn't believe how lucid he was. And that same day, as he was going out the door, he said, 'I see your husband is finishing painting the south side of the house, finally.' I'll bet he knew more than one secret about the people in this town."

Deb frowned. "Cut it out, Pat. The guy's dead, for goodness sake."

Pat nodded agreeably and took another sip of her coffee. Deb shifted in her chair, seeming to shake off the pall that had dropped over them.

"So what's on the agenda for today?" Deb asked.

Suddenly, the door to the coffeehouse pushed open, letting in a rush of cold air, along with five strangers.

Even as a newcomer to Ashland, Pat could tell that these folks were not locals. Dressed in layers of clothes, they looked like they were from another world—a fact that was confirmed when one of them strode up to the counter and said, "Please, am looking for Joe? Is he here?"

Pat and Deb looked at each other, listening to the stranger's words but pretending not to. "Who are these women?" Pat whispered.

"They must not know," Deb whispered back—although it evidently was not enough of a whisper, because the woman turned and looked straight into Deb's eyes.

"You know Joe?" she asked, in a heavily accented voice. "Vhere he is?"

Deb and Pat had inadvertently stepped into the spotlight of the Black Cat—and it was not a spotlight they wanted to be in.

"Well," Pat said, standing up, "why don't you get your cup of coffee and come sit with us?"

And with a pulling up of a few chairs, it all began.

6

Chapter Three

THE WOMAN WHO HAD ASKED ABOUT JOE SMILED HESITANTLY AT PAT AND DEB AND then turned and spoke rapidly in an oddly lilting language to the other women in her group. They walked together up to the counter, where one small woman pulled out a handmade billfold from her large purse and squinted at a travelers check.

As the women ordered by pointing and smiling at the server, Deb whispered, "The language sounds Slavic—maybe Polish or Russian. What do you think?"

Pat shrugged and then sighed—she knew now that her day would not be filled with watercolors down by the shore. Looking around, Pat realized the regular crowd of professors from Northland College, students, retirees, and farmers were just as intrigued by the women as she and Deb were. But as the women got their coffee, the quiet conversations gradually began again—their Wisconsinite niceties wouldn't allow their eavesdropping to be too obvious.

Pat stood and smiled as the women approached the table. "Hello," she welcomed them. "I'm Pat Kerry, and this is my friend Deb Linberg. And you are?"

The leader of the group pushed off her coat and sat down heavily on the chair; the other four watched and then did the same. "I'm Anastasia, and this is my sister, Helga, and Elizabeth, called Babe, and Katrina, and Sonja. Thank you for letting us sit. Forgive my rudeness, but do you know our Joe? He was supposed to meet us at airport in Minnea ... Minneapolis—that is right way to speak it, yes? But vhen he no come, and ve could not reach him

7

on telephone, ve finally rented automobile and came here. Vhat a trip! This U.S. is big, like Russia!"

Deb kicked Pat under the table, causing Pat to blurt "Ouch!"; then she asked, "Oh, are you from Russia?"

"Yah ... yes, ve come from St. Petersburg, my sister and I. Do you know ... o ... others from Moscow? And so exciting. None of us been to your vonderful country before. But everyone so friendly. Our English not so good, but ..." Anastasia's voice trailed off, and the other women looked at each other anxiously. "Joe," Anastasia continued. "Joe Abramov. You know him, yes? Has something happened to him?"

Pat turned to Deb and nodded for her to take the lead. It always seemed to be on the pastor to share bad news with families, and she was on leave from giving bad news to relations, after all.

"Are you related ... to Joe, I mean?" Deb asked.

"Yes, well, my sister and I are his ... sisters. Not others."

"I'm afraid we don't have good news for you." Deb reached across the table and took Anastasia's hand. "You see, Joe died five days ago."

"Died! Vhat?"

Upon seeing her stricken expression, the other women spoke to her in rapid Russian, and what Deb and Pat assumed to be questions came faster and got louder and louder. Anastasia held up her hands, waving the other women to quiet down, as she said, "Yes, yes, wait, wait ..." They looked at Deb, and Anastasia continued. "Vhat ... happened?"

"I'm afraid we don't actually know what happened," Pat said gently. She pointed to the building across the street. "He was found in his apartment, right there."

Visibly shaken, Anastasia translated and the noise around the table rose again.

"How could this be?" Anastasia's sister, Helga, wailed. "Vhat vill ve do now?"

Grabbing Kleenex from her purse, Pat passed tissues to the women. She couldn't even imagine their situation—coming to a strange country and learning that your loved one had died. "Is there someone else we can call for you?" she asked kindly.

Anastasia slumped in her chair dejectedly. "He sent for us. Assured us of new life. I so vanted to see him again. Now ..." Shakily, she picked up her cup and took a drink of coffee. The others watched her, silently now, and Helga with tears streaming down her face.

Pat felt a nudge under the table. Deb was giving that "Help me out, here" look.

Anastasia slumped in her chair, obviously upset and exhausted. "He offered us new life. He promised," she mumbled, as tears ran down her face. "Vhere vill ve go?"
She looked around, as if for an answer. The other women held each other as they wept, but Anastasia sat alone. In sympathy, Pat patted her hand.

Deb, in her take-charge attorney voice said, "Don't worry. We will help you."

Pat shot her a dirty look. *You must have someone else in mind*, she thought, regretting the inevitable loss of her cherished free time.

"Joe had a brother—well, he must be your brother, too, Anastasia—nearby in Hurley. Jacob."

"Yah," Anastasia said, blowing her nose. "We do have Jacob. But he no at home. Ve no could get him on telephone."

"Well, let's just take this one step at a time," Deb soothed. She whipped out her cell phone and asked firmly, "Now, what was that number?" As she waited for Jacob to answer her call, Deb's thoughts wandered to her daughter, Julia, who was spending her high school senior year studying in Madrid as a foreign exchange student. Saying good-bye to Julia in September had been tough; Deb realized wistfully that although Julia was to be gone just ten months, she would return just in time to pack up and go to college.

Julia was Deb's youngest daughter, and Deb was proud to have "survived" the teenage years of Julia—and her two sisters before her—relatively unscathed. The last few years with Julia had been hard on both of them. Now, the distance had provided a new perspective that helped them appreciate each other. If Julia were here, she likely would be impatient with her mother's efforts to help these women. *"Oh, Mom,"* Deb could hear her saying, *"you're always taking everyone else's side."*

She was brought back from her reverie by the sound of a woman's voice on the other end of the line.

"Hello. My name is Deb Linberg; I'm calling from Ashland.

9

May I speak with Jacob Abramov?"

"He's not here right now," the woman responded, "but I expect him back in a few days. May I take a message? I am his wife, Alice."

"I'm calling from the Black Cat Coffeehouse here in Ashland," Deb explained. "Please accept my sympathy on the loss of your brother-in-law. I'm actually sitting here with two of your sisters-in-law, Anastasia and Helga, who've just arrived in town. They came looking for Joe, not knowing of his death. They will need to find out about the funeral plans."

"Jacob's sisters are here in this country? In Ashland? I can't believe it!" Alice responded incredulously.

They say they are his sisters from Russia," Deb replied calmly. "We don't know them, but here they are, and we don't actually know what to do."

"Tell them to stay put, and I'll be there in half an hour!" Alice responded excitedly.

Deb grinned, her smile clearly showing her relief. "That would be just great. My friend, Pat, and I will wait here with them until you arrive."

Pat touched Deb's arm to get her attention and said softly, "Tell her they've brought three others with them."

"Do you happen to have a van?" Deb said into the phone. "Because I think you're going to need it."

After hanging up the phone, Deb walked up to the counter and handed three dollars to Sam, the barista, to cover the refills on the mugs. Seeing that fresh goodies had just arrived from the Ashland Baking Company across the street, she ordered a tray with an assortment of cranberry-cinnamon muffins, lemon poppy-seed scones, and onion bagels (her personal favorite) with a side of cream cheese. *While I'm waiting.*

Deb looked back at the table as she waited for her order. The two sisters, Anastasia and Helga, appeared to be about her own age. *Fiftyish*, she thought. She wondered if Anastasia was the older of the two, as Helga seemed to look to her sister for guidance. Slight of stature like their brother, Joe, they had dark hair and dark eyes. Both women had wonderfully strong facial features: high cheekbones, strong noses, and wide lips. Deb thought such features went together better on Helga. *I wouldn't exactly call her pretty, but*

10

she's beautiful—yes, a classic Russian woman. The other three—she'd forgotten their names already—were definitely younger. Although not obviously in their twenties, they weren't forty either. *Hard to tell much about them,* she thought, as they sat quietly talking to each other in Russian.

"Deb, here's your order," Sam called to her, breaking into her reverie.

"Oh, thanks." She scrambled through her pockets for her billfold. *Now where did I put that darn thing?* Finding it back on the table, she smiled at Sam and paid for the food. *Am I going to have to get a beeper on that billfold, just to keep from losing it?* Deb carried the pastry-laden tray back to the table.

Just as they were finishing the goodies, a harried-looking woman walked swiftly into the Black Cat and looked around until she spotted the Russian women.

"I just can't believe it!" she exclaimed as she hurried over and hugged the sisters.
"You're really here. When I had that call from..." She looked around, questioningly. "Deb, is it? I thought, what kind of crank call is this? But here you are—and how on earth?" She hugged each sister again, and tears sprang up in all their eyes. "But never mind that," she said, "I'm just glad you're here. And these women came with you?" she added, smiling at Babe, Katrina, and Sonja.

"These are good friends from back home, Babe, Katrina, and Sonja," Anastasia said politely, pointing in turn at the women around the table.

"Let's get your stuff," Alice said. She turned to Deb. "Thank you for watching out for my sisters-in-law. Can I pay you for the treats?"

"Not at all," Deb replied, heartened by the warmth of family ties. "Just let us know when Joe's funeral service is, and if there is anything we can do to help." She wrote down her phone number and gave it to Alice. Then the women noisily gathered up their belongings and left together, a gaggle of shared grief and relief.

The two women sat in the quiet of a regular coffeehouse morning for a moment. Deb turned to Pat. "So what's on your agenda for today?"

Pat just smiled, amused by her friend's insistence that she maintain focus even during a sabbatical.

Chapter Four

WHILE DEB AND PAT WAITED A MOMENT TO LET THEMSELVES ENJOY THE QUIET OF THE moment, Pat's thoughts went back to how she found herself in this coffeehouse in the first place.

Several weeks prior to that morning in the Black Cat, the bishop's secretary walked out of her boss's office, quietly closing the door behind her. Pat looked at the bishop from across his desk. This office was comfortable yet functional, the kind of room Pat would have loved for her own office, complete with antique rugs and books stacked on shelves and piled on the floor.

Bishop Peter Anderson was a good-looking middle-aged man, with a full head of white hair and a trim body, courtesy of his going to the gym three times a week.

"Pat, I don't know how you do it," he started pleasantly, picking up and playing with his rimless glasses, "but once again you've turned around a church council, hired a new secretary, and managed to get them to like you while doing it. I congratulate you. I think Pastor Steve will now have a good chance of keeping that congregation healthy."

"Ah," Pat said, and then as the bishop glanced up from his glasses with a knowing look, she smiled ruefully, surprised at how restless she felt upon hearing his praise. "Thanks."

He returned the smile and put down his glasses. "So that brings us, once again, to reassigning you to a new parish. But Pat, I must say, although your work has been excellent, you're not your usual enthusiastic, let-me-at-them self. You're not the same Pat I

13

saw a year ago." Leaning forward, he asked, "Anything you want to talk about?"

She paused for a moment, wondering if this kind man could possibly understand what she was feeling—this man who, in all his life, seemed to know what he wanted to do ... and had done it. Pat didn't even understand her feelings herself. She liked what she did, and she was good at it. What was she thinking?

"I'm sensing that not only are you glad to be done with this call, but you have been avoiding this meeting about starting another," the bishop added gently.

Pat looked up from her hands; her expression was guarded. "How could you possibly know that?" she asked.

"Well, you did cancel out on me two times already. It doesn't take a prophet to figure out something is going on with you. Where's the Pat I know, the one who can't stop talking about what she's been doing, what she's dreaming of next?"

Abashed, Pat looked down at her hands. "I do go on some, don't I?" She paused for a moment, letting the silence drift around them, and then added, "I know it sounds silly when there are pastors, especially women, who wait and pray for a parish. But I can't help feeling I've been there, done that." *So there*, Pat thought, mentally nodding her head. *I said it*. The words were out. And to her great relief at her honesty with the bishop, they filled the small room like a cool breeze.

The bishop smiled thinly. ."And your husband, Mitchell, is...?"

"Oh, he's just fine. Working, golfing, not ... it's not that or the kids. It's just ..." *How unlike me*, she thought, startled. *The bishop was listening and fully present. He really was a good man.*

"You have other things that do fire you up?" the bishop asked.

She listed the things to which she gave her spare time— "Quilting, reading, watercolor painting, refinishing antique furniture, and my two grandbabies—"—a normal kind of leisure-time list.

Tilting his head to the side, as if listening to more than her words, he continued, "Yes, but are you enjoying your work and play?"

She blinked, surprised by his question. "Well, I suppose," Pat said, and suddenly let out a small chuckle. "Actually, I suppose I'm bored to tears with it."

He sat back and chuckled with her. There was something contagious and real about his laugh. "Then maybe it's time you looked for something less boring. We wouldn't want you tearing up every time you are at a meeting, would we?"

Her brow furrowed slowly. "I do enjoy my work, you know. It just seems like the problems are all the same, and I am there to fix whatever they are. Sweep up the mess. And all I really need is a good smile, a prayer, stick-to-itiveness, and ... well ... common sense to get the job done. She sighed. It seems so ...'"

"What I have seen you do with troubled churches is fine work, Pat—not just anyone can do it. You have a real gift for working with problems in parishes, so I don't want you to misunderstand this next question. Is there something else you feel called to do? A doctorate? A book you want to write? A mission you've always wanted to go on?"

Pat shrugged. "Gee whiz, I don't know. Never had time to think about it."

The bishop nodded understandingly. He clasped his hands together as he leaned closer to her, his tone growing serious. "We all feel that way at a certain age, you know. The need becomes really strong to do all that we are called to do and to live up to our full potential. Otherwise, like those antique furniture pieces you like to restore, everything starts loosening up, dry rot sets in, and we start to wonder who we really are."

"Yes," she said simply, "but that wouldn't have been you, Bishop, and what am I to *do*? The kids have their own lives now. Mitchell is happy. I'm good at my work. It's just that——"

"It's just that you're too good at what you do. There is no chaos left in it. Too easy, perhaps?" He looked at her intently, his blue eyes filled with sympathy and just a little twinkle. "But isn't there something, somewhere, you want to do or to be? Something you never had the time or freedom for until now?"

Pat stared blankly at him. "Frankly, I'm tired. I can't even *think* with enthusiasm about doing anything. When I was in seminary, my best friend, Deb, was going to law school, and we were going to change the world—she as a judge, fighting injustice, and I ..." Pat leaned back in her chair, smiling. "I was going to be a bishop and change the Church."

Peter threw back his head and laughed, and Pat wondered,

15

not for the first time, why, whenever she was being her most truthful, people found her so amusing. "I guess that I never really fit the profile of 'pastor,'" Pat explained. "Mitchell always called me his silly little crusader—his way of justifying my quirkiness of thinking I could save the world; something he loved me for but just didn't understand, Pat thought." Peter nodded, encouraging her to continue. "And the kids? Martin just accepted me for what I was—his crazy mom, who maybe could pull a rabbit out of her hat. But my daughter, Jane, was a different story. One day, Jane and I were walking. 'Mom,' she said to me. 'I can't believe you really do—you actually think you can change things just by giving your coat to that woman?' I never even tried to explain the look I saw in that woman's eye as she huddled in that door way. She was no cute child that someone would take care of. But she had been someone's child, once. Embarrassed, I had stopped as Jane was busy telling me of her latest corporate conquest and put my old jacket over the woman's shoulders and walked away. The woman looked frightened, then confused, and then astonished. It was an old coat anyway. But I knew I wouldn't hear the end of it from my daughter. Just another example of crazy Mom. 'Why did you do that? Honestly, Mom. Give money to the coat drive. That would be the sensible thing to do. But your own coat? Now you'll freeze before we get to the restaurant!' She thought of me as an easy mark."

Pat shook her head somewhat wearily, as she continued her explanation. "I guess I'm not very realistic or sensible or even logical. Maybe," she said, as if she had sudden clarity, "I'm not happy trying to be what I'm not."

The bishop put on his glasses and ran his fingers through his hair, signaling the end of their talk. "No, you really aren't very realistic or logical sometimes, but then, neither was Jesus, was he? But he didn't try to be someone he wasn't. Maybe you need to take some time off—go paint or write a great mystery or just sit for a while. You know we will always find something for you. Whatever else you are, you are a good pastor."

Pat nodded in agreement.

They chatted a few minutes longer—about their families and the new hymnal but without the closeness from a moment before.

As Pat rose and walked to the door, she looked back to see

16

Peter, smiling and shaking his head as he murmured, "A bishop."

Except I wasn't making a joke. She realized she was a little miffed as she walked out to the parking lot. I really was going to try to change the Church! The dear Lord knows it needs a good airing out. I'll ask for leave-of-call paperwork tomorrow.

And she did.

Chapter Five

Still thinking about her talk with the Bishop, Pat entered her townhouse and looked around. The sunlight streaming through the windows seemed to highlight the dust on the antique end table. She threw off her coat, walked into the kitchen, and picked up a dust rag. Her personal calendar was on the counter, opened to this day, and as she glanced at it in passing, she had a strange sense of awareness of the mundane details of her life.

Today was Wednesday—that usually meant a "church night" filled with a variety of activities. There would be confirmation classes, Wednesday night school and supper for the little kids, meetings of one or more of the church committees, and then choir practice. But then every day was filled to the brim with activities: a Bible study on Thursday morning, followed by the women's group executive board. On Friday, a men's coffee and work group, and then the president of the council would be in to talk about building problems. It would be a rush, of course, to make sure her sermon was ready for Sunday. And she'd fit in one or more unhappy wives or husbands and a visit or two to a hospital. Another week of church work.

On Saturday, she would have lunch with her old friend, Christine, but Christine would talk about all the trips she and Ron had been taking, along with the adventures and joys of traveling first class.

Peter had said, *Isn't there something you've always wanted to do but never had the time?*

Pat tossed the dust rag on the chair, then reluctantly picked it up and dusted the table, knowing if she didn't do it now she would have to do it sometime. It was important to keep the house up. As she returned the rag to the kitchen, she stooped to pick up yesterday's paper that Mitchell had left by his chair the night before. *Might as well put this in the recycling,* Pat thought.

She was about to toss the paper in the recycling bin when an article caught her eye on the front of the human interest section—a 58 year old woman about her age—two years younger, in fact—had quit her job, sold her house and all of her belongings, and joined the Peace Corps. For the last year she had been helping children in Uganda learn to read and had lived in a village in a small hut and written a novel in her evenings, which was now to be published.

"I could have never done this when I was young," the woman had told the reporter. "Everyone thinks the Peace Corps is for kids right out of college, and there are a lot of them doing it, but I believe this village needed me, an older woman, who could use the things I had learned in the past to help them. My book is not really about this experience; it's a mystery book. At my age, I've decided to do the things I want. And that's the kind of book I read, so that's what I wrote." The reporter went on to say that the book was refreshingly silly and an unexpectedly delightful read. "A good gift book for that reader in your life," the reporter had noted.

Pat tossed the paper into the bin. *"They needed me."* What an idea, she thought, walking to the closet to hang up her coat. She caught a glimpse of herself in the hall mirror and stared at the woman who looked back at her. She saw a woman of average height with more around the waist and hips than was healthy. And frown lines. *Where did they come from?* Leaning closer, she looked into her eyes. Sad? No, that wasn't it, but she definitely had seen more sorrow than most women her age. And her eyes were dull. *Where's the sparkle that used to be in my eyes? Could I sell everything and move to a faraway village, just for the adventure?*

At the back of Pat's mind flashed a time when she was driving, and she'd just stopped the car along the road and cried—cried for no reason. She'd almost been afraid to drive the car for fear of whether she would care if she—no, she cautioned herself, *best not to think of that.* She stared more intently into the mirror. "Isn't there something you've always wanted to do?" she asked her reflection.

Pat thought of Deb, her friend for thirty-five years. They knew more about each other than their husbands and kids knew about them. As best friends, they'd raised their kids together. They'd been there for each other through babies' fevers and chicken pox and husbands' coming (and going). They'd been friends before cell phones were even thought of, and they had to stretch the cord on the phone as far as it would reach, so they could talk and still make dinner for their respective families; friends through picnics and camping, through weight gains and losses.

I was there when she married Marc, thought Pat fondly, as she recalled their history. *It was a new beginning for her and the girls. She was there when I was ordained. I laughed out loud when she finally got her law degree, refusing her daughter's advice to sit out the ceremony because she was nine months pregnant. And she cried with me when my pop died.*

Suddenly missing her friend, Pat picked up the phone and dialed Deb's number.

After Pat told Deb about her restless thoughts, Deb replied, "Come live up here for a while. You and Mitch could fix up one of these old houses. You could paint the lake, and he could paint the outside of the house. And if you really feel guilty about not helping people every minute of the day," she gently chided, "I'm sure there are kids here who need a reading buddy or lots of other things."

It was insane; a silly imagining. "What would I tell people I was doing?" Pat asked.

Deb laughed. "Tell them you're writing a mystery."

"Of course, I could at least ask Mitchell about it," Pat said, feeling her way around the idea as it grew. Just thinking about how they would go about it would be a nice little break.

"Don't just daydream about," Deb insisted. "Get a 'for sale' sign and put it out in the yard. See what happens."

It was crazy; simply crazy.

Still, Pat gave a lot of thought to Deb's suggestion. *How like her to be so generous. A gift of a place and a time where no one listens to me but the waves on the big lake as I walk on its stony shore. A place where I can bring out my brushes and drink coffee every morning, and read the paper from front to back. Where no cell phone connects me to someone who needs my sympathy or*

21

advice, or calls me to judge whether the women's group should really be having a bingo fund-raiser. No one at all to need me, except maybe the big lake herself, to tell her how beautiful she is in my watercolors. Pat sniffed and blew her nose.

After speaking to her friend on the phone, Deb picked up her journal and wrote. *Ashland really is a place where I felt at home from the first moment I gazed at the big lake, the "Tall Water," on the drive into town nearly thirteen years ago. Marc and I moved to this sleepy little college town of eight thousand, located right on the south shore of Lake Superior at the base of Chequamegon Bay, in search of new adventure and a progressive place to raise our two babies, Julia and Eric. We found all of our requirements in one town: big water for sailing, some intellectual stimulation, a place where everyone knows your face, scenic beauty and a place rich in history—a town that knows where it came from.*

We are both fortunate to have careers that transfer almost anywhere. Marc a family doctor who loves the challenge of working in underserved areas. His Peace Corps experience in this country, he calls it. Except the town of Ashland is anything but underserved. His first practice didn't suit his style. Now he commutes around the Bayfield peninsula twenty-five miles north to the Red Cliff Indian Reservation every day.

I started a family law office at home to be available for the kids and to try to limit my time at work. Strange thing about home offices. As much as it is charming and convenient to greet clients on the back deck on a warm summer's day, it becomes harder and harder, as time goes on, to close the door to the office at the end of the day. The work is always there, calling like a siren, constantly beckoning. So when the opportunity arose to join with another local attorney and set up a joint practice at the center of town, I jumped at it. And I still have no regrets.

Chapter Six

ABOUT THE SAME TIME AS PAT AND DEB SAT RELAXING IN THE BLACK CAT COFFEEHOUSE after meeting the Russian sisters, the phone rang loudly in the nearby Ashland office of Detective Gary LeSeur. He swung his long legs off the desk as he reached over to pick up. "LeSeur here."

"Officer Marie here. Sorry to bother you, but I have to report a dead body found home alone here in Ashland. Joseph Abramov, a fifty- seven-year-old male, with no obvious cause of death."

"Yeah—go on—really? What does it look like? Is it a murder? Any signs of a forced entry? What do you know about the deceased?" Quickly, LeSeur reached for something to write on and began to scribble some notes as he talked.

"No sign of a struggle; no sign of a forced entry. Don't know anything about the guy, Chief. It all looks okay, I guess. Probably the poor guy just had a heart attack or something. But you know, it was so neat in there. So ... I don't know much. Anyway, I called the coroner and she's on her way."

"Don't move anything or touch anything. I'll be there in five," LeSeur said with authority.

LeSeur's mind raced as he quickly assumed his investigator mode and shifted smoothly into automatic pilot. He formed a plan of action in his head. The questions came easily for him now.

It had been twenty-three years since LeSeur had graduated in the top of his police officer training program and subsequently joined the Ashland Police Department. At first, he was assigned to routine patrol—back when life was even simpler in Ashland,

23

the town where he had grown up in a happy childhood filled with strong family ties, sports, music, and church. All six of the LeSeur kids eventually went away to college and became professionals; all of them came back to this bucolic little town to get married and raise their kids.

Drop-dead handsome with a copper complexion—compliments of his Indian mother—Gary's middle-aged body was still fit, and his face had an ever-present smile. He had quickly earned the trust and respect of his peers on the force and in the community that knew and loved him. His knowledge of the people and places in town gave him a leg up over the others on the force. Gary had been initially assigned to bike patrol in the summer due to his familiarity and rapport with the public, but those days were done.

Investigations came easy to him. He soon earned a reputation as an ace at solving the minor crimes that happened in all small towns: vandalism of lawn ornaments, petty thefts, and an occasional auto theft that usually turned out to be a teenager's joyride, as well as the tragic reports of abuse and neglect of children.

Once, when there was major vandalism at the local elementary school, he was able to get to the bottom of it fairly quickly. More recently, he had been a leader in the crusade against the slow influx of drug trade that was creeping into the community—a place that he had once thought of as "Mayberry-like."

Gary had grown to accept the hard parts of his job. His work was taxing at times because underneath his tough exterior, he had a real compassion for people of all stripes. He despaired at the ways that humans could find to destroy their lives—often due to alcohol and drugs.

Now, Gary placed the phone slowly back in its cradle. *Joe Abramov—dead*, Gary thought. *Poor old guy—he was colorful, if nothing else.* If Gary were being less charitable, he might have referred to Joe as a crackpot—someone who had been part of the local landscape for many years now but about whom the police department had received a few complaints from frightened townies—about the wacky guy with the eye patch who talked to everyone and accused the CIA of conspiring against him.

Gary put on his windbreaker and moved quickly out into the

24

night. As he drove to the scene, his mind conjured memories of the deceased. Gary had talked with Joe on several occasions and quickly determined that the guy was harmless—half-cracked from the war, for sure, but all talk. Most people, in time, had learned to either ignore or be amused by Joe's rants.

And now the guy is dead. Gary ticked off a mental checklist as he considered what could have happened to Joe:

- ❑ Mentally ill: Joe could have been suicidal, and no one would have known. He could have just decided he'd had enough of his war memories and ended it all himself.
- ❑ Chain smoker: Joe's habit could have caused a stroke or heart attack, and he wouldn't have been able to call for help if he was alone.
- ❑ Choking episode: Joe lived alone—if he was choking, no one could help him.

Yet there was something in Officer Marie's voice that gave Gary pause. The body, she'd said, appeared to be intact, and there was no sign of a struggle or forced entry. Still, she had implied that something just didn't seem right about the whole thing. *What was it she had said, exactly?* Gary looked down at his hastily scribbled notes. There it was: "Don't know, Chief. It all looks okay, I guess. Maybe the poor guy just had a heart attack or something. But you know, it's so neat in there. So ... I don't know. Anyway, I called the coroner, Ruth Epstein, and she's on her way."

If this was an unnatural event—Gary had trouble even imagining the word murder—then he knew that his life was about to be a whole lot busier.

Down the street from Deb's home, the phone rang several times, interrupting the repartee going on in Joel and Ruth Epstein's kitchen. Usually when they had company around the table and were engaged in light-hearted banter, as they were this evening, Ruth let the answering machine pick up.

Tonight, however, she was expecting a call from her son, Adam, in New York City, letting her know the results of his audition with the Blue Man Group—Adam was hoping for his first real break as he tried to hit the "big time" following college.

To Ruth's disappointment, the voice on the phone was not Adam's. Instead, it was Marie Brownstone, Ashland's only patrolwoman.

Not another dead body, Ruth thought. As coroner in a small town, it was her job to pronounce bodies dead. She glanced at the gathering of AFS parents around her table, all telling stories about their hosting experiences with foreign exchange students. She took the phone upstairs and gathered pen and paper to write down the address.

Being coroner of the town had been a lark at first, fueled by her medical training as a nurse, interest in forensic medicine, and desire for any adventure she could find. She had campaigned for the coroner position several years previous after becoming fed up with the incompetence of the previous coroner.

Ruth knew she was well suited to the demands of the job. Introverted, she sometimes preferred working with bodies that couldn't talk back. Conscientious, smart, and calm, she was not bothered by blood and guts or by the sight of dead people.

Ruth and her husband, Joel, had moved to Ashland nearly thirty years ago as newlyweds. They had raised their family here and become pillars in the community—a remarkable feat, considering they both had come from urban backgrounds. Ruth was a Jewish agnostic; Joel had grown up on the West Coast. She and Joel had met at college in Ohio and been together ever since. World travelers, they had put down roots in this provincial town, bringing the world to the town over the years through their hosting of nearly twenty AFS students in their home.

Ruth walked slowly downstairs and smiled stoically at her happy guests, all warmed with delectable homemade desserts and after-dinner coffee.

"I'm sorry to do this," she said, "but I've just been called to a possible suspicious death scene." I

Ruth's guests stared at their hostess with looks that ranged from awe to horror, amazed and incredulous that someone as down to earth as Ruth could do the job as coroner. It was the closest to being in the presence of celebrity as one could achieve in Ashland.

Ruth put on her red wool coat, retrieved her coroner's

26

bag from the closet, and quickly exited the house. Sydney, Ruth's exuberant Australian shepherd, stared longingly out the window after her, seemingly incredulous that his one true love would leave the house without him.

Ruth drove the five blocks down Chapple Avenue to Joe's apartment building, and when she arrived at the scene just a few minutes later, the yellow tape was already placed around the entire apartment building. Several police cars and an ambulance were parked outside, as well as the fire chief's car.

A small crowd had begun to gather, drawn by the sirens that had pierced the late autumn evening solitude of this sleepy town. Officer Marie was standing outside, waiting expectantly for Ruth's arrival. Detective LeSeur was in the crowd, talking to the neighbors. *Standard procedure*, Ruth thought approvingly. Sam, the barista from the Black Cat, was there, concern and grief clearly etched on his face.

"You're gonna want to be careful about breathing too deeply when you go in," Marie offering in greeting. "It smells pretty bad in there."

Ruth walked quickly up the stairs with Officer Marie, gathering her thoughts and her professional composure as she went. As she opened the door to Joe's apartment, she was immediately met by the overpowering odor of decomposing flesh. *This starts to get old fast*, she thought, reaching into her bag for the jar of Vicks and putting a dab in her nostrils. And then she saw the body, which she immediately recognized as Joe Abramov. Were it not for the decomposition, Joe might have appeared to be resting comfortably in an overstuffed armchair—he was wearing Bermuda shorts, a short-sleeved dress shirt, and black shoes and socks. Unfortunately, he "rested" in close proximity to a small space heater—the room felt warm, probably between 75 and 80 degrees, Ruth guessed—and she could tell that Joe had been dead for some time. She realized it was common knowledge in Ashland that Joe had a few screws loose. She took out a notebook and pen, walked over to the body, and looked at her slim silver Timex watch. *9:25 p.m.* The time of death was always the time the coroner first pronounced the person dead.

Ruth went through the motions. She inspected Joe's body without unduly disturbing it or undressing it. She was struck by the neatness of his clothing. There did not appear to be any visible marks on the body. She looked closely to see if she could detect any gross signs of a bullet hole. There was no blood and no sign of any tearing of his clothing. Joe's abdomen appeared swollen, and his face was discolored, with freshly dried froth around his mouth.

Reaching into his right rear pants pocket, Ruth pulled out a worn brown wallet. Gesturing to the expectant officer, Ruth motioned for Marie to assist her in going through the contents. Looking inside the wallet, she found a couple dollars and twenty cents in change; some old receipts from the County Market grocery store; and an old military ID with a photograph of a much younger Joseph Abramov. Officer Marie held out her hands as Ruth deposited the money and papers into them and then slid the contents of the wallet into a manila envelope. She sealed the envelope carefully.

Looking around, Ruth observed that the apartment was neat. Aside from ashtrays brimming with cigarette butts, there was no clutter, no dirty dishes. *Strange. Not the kind of orderly environment one would expect from a mentally ill person,* Ruth thought.

Ruth pulled out her digital Canon PowerShot and walked slowly through the apartment, room by room, meticulously snapping photos of the scene from every conceivable angle. She looked through everything in each room, carefully opening every drawer, cupboard, and the medicine cabinet, searching for pill bottles.

She turned to Marie, who stood at the doorway, as if waiting for Ruth to decide whether or not to order an autopsy. Ruth knew that the county would have to pay if an autopsy were ordered. There was no question in her mind about the proper course of action.

"Well, he's dead; no question about that. But based on appearances, I have no idea what caused this death. We'll have to send him south for an autopsy at Regina Medical Center in Hastings, Minnesota, since he died unattended at home." Ruth gently covered Joe's body with the white sheet she pulled out of her bag. Carefully, she catalogued the contents of the wallet and placed it into her coroner's bag.

Pulling out her cell phone, she speed-dialed the local undertaker across the street. "Stan, it's Ruth Epstein. I have a body to go to the morgue. It's 208 Chapple Avenue."

She waited patiently until the director and his assistant

28

arrived with the gurney a few minutes later. The two men carefully placed the sheet-wrapped body into a body bag and placed it on the gurney. Ruth walked wearily down the stairs, accompanying the body, making sure that there was no interference in the chain of custody. She would have to go with the body to the local hospital, where she would do a full inspection of the man's remains in the morgue. Ruth made a mental note to call the pathologist after she got home to set up a time for the autopsy.

I believe I've had enough of this business, she mused. *After the first hundred dead bodies, the glamour has faded.* Ruth decided she would ask Kathy Barker, her deputy, if she was ready to take over the job.

When Ruth finally arrived home again, her guests had left and her kitchen was empty. Only Sydney, the eager Australian shepherd, was watching for her from the window.

Earlier that same evening, Pat and Mitchell Kerry and Deb and Marc Linberg were eating dinner in the Linberg kitchen.

"Okay, but you've got to admit it's really odd. Come on, you guys, really. Don't you think?" Pat reached across the table for the salad as she spoke, looking longingly at the mashed potatoes.

Mitchell raised his eyes at Marc as he passed the platter of grilled whitefish. It was a look that the two men reserved over the years of their friendship for when they thought their wives were acting ditzy.

"What exactly looks odd about the situation?" Mitchell asked. "Logically, the guy was at risk because he smoked and drank. He lived alone in an apartment and was found dead in his chair. What could be more real?" Turning to Marc, he continued, "Can you pull out another beer, Marc? I think this is going to be a two-brew night."

"You bet." Standing, Marc remarked, "Anyway, it's sad, but I'm with Mitch."

No surprise in that, Pat thought, mentally shrugging. She glanced over at Deb; the guys didn't notice.

"The guy was an accident waiting to happen," Marc called

29

out as he returned from the kitchen. "Here, Mitch." He placed a beer in front of his friend and sat down. Marc finally relaxed. "Pass the salad, will you?"

No wonder he's so skinny, Pat thought enviously.

"There's more to it than that," Deb protested. "Why now? Why sitting in his chair? It's not just sad, it's a little spooky. Maybe I'm reacting to his being alone when he died. May it never happen to me to be alone when I die," she added, looking up in silent prayer. "But it just seems so staged."

"Could have been a suicide," Mitchell piped in between mouthfuls. "Like you said, he was a loner and a little crazy. Maybe he just decided to check out."

Pat shook her head. "It doesn't wash. He was talking about traveling. He had just gotten a new glass eye so he wouldn't have to wear the patch," she continued, ticking off on her fingers. "And what about the lottery ticket? It was all over the Black Cat this morning that the winning ticket was announced, but no one claimed it yet because Joe had it."

"Lottery ticket?"

"Yes, didn't you hear? A few years back he won part of a lottery—you knew that, right? But everyone is saying he won again."

"Oh, by 'everyone,' you mean everyone at the coffeehouse? Of course, the Black Cat is such a reliable source of information." Marc sighed and wiped his mouth with his napkin. "Aren't these the same people who are convinced the president is a front for the CIA? The guy already won a lottery; what are the odds of winning two? You girls are so dramatic sometimes."

"Stranger things have happened," Pat replied. Then, smiling sheepishly, she continued, "Well, not many, but it could have happened, couldn't it?"

"Actually, each time the odds are calculated by the numbers in that particular lottery. So it doesn't really matter if he won one before," Mitchell pointed out.

"Do you want to know what I think?" Marc asked, leaning his elbows on the table. "I think you, Pat, have all this time on your hands because you're on sabbatical, and you, Deb, want to have an adventure with her. So you're imagining this for fun. Let the poor guy rest in peace." Turning, he asked, "What do you think, Mitch?"

"I think its time for dessert, not 'just deserts.' Who wants ice cream?" he quipped, dodging a spousal bullet.

They all laughed and settled in, as only old friends can do.

Chapter Seven

THE NEXT MORNING, DEB GOT UP AT SIX O'CLOCK, AS SHE USUALLY DID, TO DO YOGA stretching and relaxing exercises with her reluctant husband. Ever since she and Marc had hosted Swami Ji, the yoga master from Nepal, in their home for a month, they had continued their practice together. *Even though he sometimes tries to get out of it, the goose.* Normally, she liked to linger in the aftermath with the feeling of deep relaxation and serenity, but today she couldn't wait to walk up the street to pick up Pat and walk the five blocks to coffee.

Entering the coffeehouse, Deb threw her coat on the chair and hurried to get her coffee. Kait, an artistic brunette with sparkling eyes and a cute smile, was working today and, as usual, she had two mugs waiting on the counter.

Deb enjoyed the feeling of living in a place where the service people knew what she wanted when she walked in the door.

The morning had been like most others for Kait. There were the usual requests for empty mugs from students, housewives, and working folk, eyes glazed over and eager for their morning shot of java to fortify them for the day. Like Deb and Pat, they were the easy ones to wait on—customers who would choose from the four pots of ready-made set out on the coffee bar.

That morning, the choices were French Roast (dark), Chilean Blend (regular), Mocha (flavored), and French Roast (decaf). One of the most creative aspects of being a barista was being in charge of choosing the flavors for the day. Kait would arrive at work each morning in the wee hours to open up and start the pots brewing.

The more time-consuming customers were the espresso and latte types who ordered from the numerous selections of handwritten entries on the overhead chalkboard. That morning, a chilly one, had been especially busy with special orders.

Brrr. It's cold today, Deb thought, as she went for the French Roast. *Almost time for the wool socks and mittens.* Joining Pat at their table, Deb smiled and started right in.

"Wait 'til you hear the latest!" She paused for a few seconds for dramatic effect, leaving Pat wondering what Deb was about to say. "I got a call last night from Anastasia. She first thanked me for writing the letter to the editor in the paper. Then she asked me if I would help her and Jacob to tie up Joe's affairs. They need a little legal advice and guidance." She watched Pat's face light up with interest as she shared this information with her. At that moment, it struck her how nice it was to see Pat taking an interest in things once again.

My best friend, thought Deb, *has been struggling with burn-out for some time, even though she wouldn't call it that.* Though they had lived hours away from each other for the past several years, distance hadn't seemed to affect the closeness they felt. They had been sisters in spirit for most of the past thirty years.

Deb knew that Pat was a delightful pastor who used her intellect and catalytic personality and charm to bring grace to the lives of her congregations. But she wondered how many times during their careers they had learned the price of healing others' situations at the expense of their own care.

Before Pat's last interim pastor job began, they had met on Madeline Island, their favorite sacred place, with a few other friends. There, they brainstormed about future life directions and made room for their dreams. They had actually talked about ways they could still save the world while saving themselves. Then, shortly thereafter, Deb watched with disappointment and helplessness as Pat once again accepted an interim position for another year.

Another year of draining her energy, Deb thought. *If she would just allow herself to take some time off, it would be really good for her and really good for the world.*

Deb had watched as Pat's joy of living had steadily shrunk. It was as if Pat's life had become black and white, when it used to be rainbows. And how Deb wished she could take a brush and paint the colors back in for her.

Thinking about her friend, Deb felt a sudden dull pain in her heart. She remembered her daughter Brenda's unexpected death several years ago now. Deb had taken a year off from work afterwards. Some people might think it was just a phrase—"having your heart broken—"—but Deb knew it was true. Deb's heart still felt a little broken when she thought of her oldest daughter, despite all the years of healing.

That wasn't the only time she had taken extended time off from work. She had also taken a year off during the first year she had moved to Ashland. She and Marc had decided that it was important to the family to have one of them at home while they all made the transition. That was a magical year of discovery of the sights and people in her new home.

Both times were times of transformation for me, remembered Deb. *I got to do anything I wanted and mostly just focus on my own needs. It was like taking the weight of the world off my shoulders and setting it down. Strangely, they were two of my best years.*

Deb reverie was broken by Pat's persistent questions. "So, are the Russian women coming to your office? What did they learn about Joe's death? Is there going to be a service?"

Deb smiled and leaned back in her chair. Her friend Pat was definitely back. "Now, you know I can't tell you anything that's confidential, but Anastasia did say to thank you, too, and said she would like to get together with us sometime. She had only met her sister-in-law once before, you know, and I think she really wants someone else to talk to. Those poor women, coming all this way." She tipped her cup to get another sip of the French Roast and then said, "Don't you wonder where Joe got the money to send for all of them?"

Pat looked at Deb in astonishment. "You mean to say that Joe sent the money for all five of them to come to America? That must have cost a fortune! I can't believe that he could possibly have had that much money—he didn't even buy his own coffee most of the time, He always wore the same clothes, and he lived in that crummy little apartment across the street. Why would he do that if he had money? He didn't have a job. Mmm, I wonder where that money came from."

Before Deb could respond, a middle-aged woman came

through the door. She pulled a scarf off her curly auburn hair and, glancing around, smiled at Deb; then went to get her coffee.

"Who's that?" Pat asked.

"It's one of the nurses from the clinic," Deb replied. "Actually, I think she's someone you'll probably want to meet."

"Oh? Why?"

"Because she is not just any nurse," Deb said. "She's the county coroner and also a neighbor of ours. She's the one who sent Joe's body to St. Paul for the autopsy."

"Well, in that case, invite her to sit with us."

Joe's death was common knowledge all over town, so when Deb asked Ashland's coroner when the body would be released, Ruth Epstein felt she wasn't breaking any confidences by discussing minor details. "I think it will be done by the end of the week," she said as she bit into a caramel roll.

"I'm representing Joe's family," Deb explained. "They're wondering about the cause of death."

Taking a sip of her coffee, Ruth sighed. "It was most likely a heart attack, I expect. Poor guy. Maybe it'll be a comfort for his family to know that he probably didn't know what hit him."

"I'm just curious," Pat said. "How can you tell a thing like that?"

"Well, in this case," Ruth explained, her mouth full of caramel roll, "it looks like he was sitting in his chair when it happened. He had a look of surprise on his face. No trying to get to the phone or anything." Turning to Deb, she said, "How is it that the family contacted you?"

"Well, we met the sisters in here when they came into town. We helped them contact their brother, Jacob."

"Can I get Anastasia's phone number from you? I'll have my assistant call the family as soon as the body is released. I'll try to give them all the details I can then. But in the meantime," she said with a stern look, "I would appreciate it if you wouldn't talk about it too much. There is a proper order to things, you know, even in a small town."

"Thank you," Deb said, relieved to learn that Joe hadn't suffered. Still, it made her a little sad. *It was a lonely and undignified way to go. But at least he wasn't really aware of it.*

Ten minutes later, Ruth was on her second cup of coffee

when she glanced at her watch. "Look at the time. I've got a 9:00." Picking up her cup, she turned to Pat. "Nice meeting you," she smiled sincerely as she put her cup in the cleanup bin. Then, retying her scarf over her curls, she walked out the door.

Deb picked up her coat. "Well, I'd like to sit some more, but I'm meeting Anastasia and her sister at my office."

After waving good-bye to Deb, Pat got up and put her seventy-five cents on the counter for a refill, then picked up the paper, looking for the article about Joe. *What a good job!* Pat thought, as she read:

Friend, neighbor, veteran
Chapple Avenue character remembered
By Karen Hollish
Staff writer

Chapple Avenue residents often noticed eye-patched Joe Abramov, who passed away unexpectedly last week at age fifty-seven, pacing in front of the area's bakery and coffee shop, giving passersby an enthusiastic morning greeting, espousing his dreams of winning the lottery, and darting into the food co-op to ask and answer one of his own favorite questions: "Who am I? I'm Harry Potter!"

Ashland local Rico Lopez remembered of Abramov, "He smoked, and he would always offer me a cigarette. He would try to speak to me in Spanish and say 'Fumar, señor?' I don't smoke cigarettes, and I always refused, but he always offered me one, and always showed that sense of humor with that saying. I came to enjoy it, and of course if he wouldn't do it, I'd be disappointed. But he never disappointed me."

At first glance, Abramov appeared to be a colorful character with a penchant for sharing his escapist fantasies and a fear of the government that seemed to verge on paranoia, but he also served two tours during the Vietnam War and earned three bronze stars. He was a regular fixture of downtown Ashland, especially at the Daily Bread, Black Cat Coffeehouse, and Chequamegon Food Co-op businesses near his Chapple Avenue home. When Abramov wasn't seen for several days, a concerned Black

Cat barista called the police, who visited Abramov's apartment and found him dead.

News of his death quickly spread through the community, and neighbors and friends built an impromptu memorial next to his home. There, one can see a handmade sign reading "Joe: rest in peace—friend, neighbor, veteran," around which friends have placed candles, flowers, artwork, lottery tickets—and cigarettes.

Abramov might have been best known for his perpetually discussed dream of winning the lottery. He planned to use the money to buy an island, where deer and alligators would be the only animals and brandy was omnipresent and where he'd wed and bed several Russian women.

But those who made more time to listen to Abramov were privy to another side of him, which was kind, compassionate, and highly intelligent, albeit scarred by his two tours in Vietnam.

"I know he suffered from post-traumatic stress disorder [PTSD], and I know it firsthand, because I do, too," said Lopez, also a Vietnam veteran. "This is a mechanism that he used to escape reality. He would speak a couple of sentences that were really very intelligent and compassionate, and then he'd go back into that odd character. I understood why he did what he did, and I accepted it as what he had to do to survive."

Inescapable past pain

Though Abramov made references to previous major life events—such as his military service and his run for Ashland mayor—many of his life details were shrouded in mystery. Only after his death have his Chapple Avenue friends learned more about him.

A graduate of Bayfield High School and later a sociology student at Ohio State University, Abramov was an American whose family believed strongly in military service, said his sister-in-law, Alice Abramov of Hurley. Alice Abramov's husband, Jacob, also served in the military, like his brother, Joe.

"It was a family that believed in patriotism, a family of engineers and military men, even in Russia," she said. "So their history of being in the military is very firmly entrenched."

Alice Abramov remembers that when her husband was called to go to

38

combat in Vietnam, brothers weren't allowed to simultaneously serve in combat situations. Seeing that his brother had a wife and child who would be affected by his going, Joe Abramov decided to volunteer, rendering his brother ineligible.

"That did interfere with their relationship for many years, because Jacob thought it was his duty to go," Alice Abramov said.

Joe Abramov distinguished himself as a friend on the battlefield.

"He was one of those people they referred to as a 'soldier's soldier,' which meant that if you were in any kind of combat situation, that's who you wanted next to you, because that was the person who could help you stay alive," Mrs. Abramov said.

When Abramov returned, he suffered from PTSD-related dissociation and could have qualified for 100 percent service-connected disability status, but he refused, denying that anything was wrong.

"He refused, I think, because he did not want to take anything from the government; he was so paranoid and so distrustful of the military," Alice Abramov said.

"Like a brother"

Though Abramov spent some of his post-service time homeless in Florida, his home, for the most part, was Ashland. He strayed from his regular Chapple Avenue spots to visit with Heike Clausen and Gabriele Schmitt, of Heike's Blumen Garden and Gabriele's German Cookies & Chocolates on Main Street, who were charmed by him.

"He stopped at least three to four times a day at the flower shop, and he bought chocolates, and he wanted to win the lottery and buy an island," Clausen remembered. "And I was supposed to be the lady who took care of the flowers on the island."

Beyond his expressed fantasies, Schmitt remembers that Abramov was very well-spoken about classic pieces of literature, like *Anna Karenina* or *Doctor Zhivago*.

Clausen also remembers him as a lonely man—she visited his apartment when he spent Christmas alone—and as a man who discouraged others from joining the military.

"My daughter, Anne—she's—thirteen—and he told her, 'Anne, you're too smart to go into the military. . Don't go into the military,'" Clausen said.

Sometimes Abramov's persistent questioning or his insistence upon early morning conversations with people waiting in the coffee line could be bothersome to Chapple Avenue-goers, who'd try to ignore him.

Luanne Johnson, a cook at the Black Cat, called Abramov a great friend, but she also remembered how his energy could become unmanageable in public situations. When rumors circulated of an impending Iraq War draft, Abramov overheard Ashland former Mayor Carl Johnson talking of how he was afraid his son could be drafted. Startled by the conversation, Abramov abruptly suggested a way that Johnson could keep that from happening.

"Joe flew off the handle and said, 'Just take his hand and smash it with a hammer. Smash it with a hammer!'" Johnson recalled. "When people heard that, everyone fled the building."

Abramov showed his friends he cared about them by weaving them into his fantasies. He promised many people posts on his island: Johnson was to be his cook, Schmitt was to feed him and his wives chocolate in bed, and Lopez would be his security guard.

Alice Abramov said she thinks her brother-in-law would be pleasantly surprised by the feelings expressed in the memorial. "I think sometimes Joe felt that no one ever really cared or noticed, and I think he would've been surprised to know how much people really did," she said.

Lopez said Abramov will be a much-missed part of the Chapple Avenue landscape. He plans on raising his veteran's flag at an upcoming ceremony and has distributed buttons that read "Remember Joe." ." He plans to maintain his memorial through Abramov's Tuesday funeral service. "This is the least I can do for a fellow veteran. I consider people like Joe my brother," Lopez said. "We gave something of ourselves by doing what society asks of us as warriors. And I look at Joe as being one of those kinds of people and a brother in that respect."

Chapter Eight

THERE WAS DEFINITELY A WINTER CHILL IN THE AIR FOR JOE'S MEMORIAL SERVICE. THE two women stood by the open grave, and as she looked up at the overcast sky, Pat could almost feel the snow in the air. *When it comes, we could be in for ten or twelve inches*, she thought.

Tall, stately oaks graced the small cemetery on the edge of town. Pat imagined that in summer, wild flowers would grow in the grass near Joe's grave—he might like that. *Of course*, Pat chided herself; *I really don't know what Joe would like. Still, he might be pleased at this turnout.*

As the rent-a-preacher droned on about a Joe she didn't recognize, Pat let her eyes move around the crowd. She was surprised at the number of mourners, most of whom jiggled from foot to foot in the cold. She noticed the Russian women—the three friends—Babe, Katrina, and Sonja, who stood bundled together with their arms around each other. Joe's sisters, Anastasia and Helga, were there, too, of course, huddled sadly together. Pat noticed for the first time that Anastasia was shorter and heavier than her sister, although both women had inherited the traditional stocky Russian build that their brothers had. Anastasia had penetrating brown eyes, high cheekbones, and—under less trying circumstances—a ready smile. She was clearly more outgoing than Helga. Now, however, she appeared to be visibly shaking.

Helga was the more conventionally attractive sister—thinner than Anastasia and with a small narrow nose and delicate features. She seemed quiet but appeared to Pat to be a rock of serenity.

Babe was a sprightly woman, standing about four foot ten. A nurse who usually dressed in bright red, she had boundless energy and passion for life. Her positive attitude was infectious and a likely source of strength to her friends during this sad time. Babe appeared to Pat to be performing ballet moves to keep herself warm during the service.

Katrina was the bravest and most adventurous of the Russian women. Fiercely independent and self-sufficient, she had left her abusive husband behind years ago to pursue a career as a linguist. She appeared to follow the service closely, more clearly able than the other women to understand every word.

Sonja appeared to be the frailest of the Russians. Dark-complected, with a medium build, she walked with a hitch in her gait, appeared to wear a constant mantle of anxiety and responsibility that etched itself in her features. Unknown to most, she had harbored a secret desire for many years that someday she would marry Joe. She held a bright blue handkerchief to her nose, constantly wiping her taut, lined face.

The brother, Jacob, whom Pat had not seen until today, stood a bit apart from the women with his wife. Pat looked at him more closely—he was heavyset, with thinning gray hair and a gray beard. If she hadn't known better, she almost might have thought it was Joe standing there, so similar were their facial features and eyes. Jacob, however, was at least ten years older. Jacob's visible grief was etched into his face. Pat recalled at that moment how Joe had volunteered to take his place in the war.

Standing by the minister were six honor-guard soldiers in dress blues, representing the army color guard, waiting to give the salute. And behind them, men of different ages from the community, some in uniform, were there to pay their final respects to a fallen mate.

There was Ernest Lopez, a gray-haired Native American Vietnam vet, who now devoted himself to making peace in the world. Next to him was James Adams, a stocky middle-aged man wearing a baseball cap, who also served in Vietnam as a medic and who had evolved into a know-it-all, left-leaning political junkie.

Ernest's son-in-law, Stuart Reuben, stood soberly nearby. Stuart was in his late twenties and had recently returned from his second tour of duty in Afghanistan. He was becoming reacquainted with his family and hometown after being discharged with honor from the Marines.

There was Lulu, a woman Pat recognized as the owner of a shop on Main Street that seemed to have stopped in time in the sixties. She was crying quietly and holding a tie-dyed hanky to her nose. Next to her was a man Pat didn't know—perhaps Lulu's husband—looking cold and a little grumpy. Then there were a few who worked at the co-op and a whole group of servers and cooks from the Black Cat, which seemed only right to Pat. And there was Bill, one of the local artists, who was always in the Black Cat, too.

Mike Williamson, the local banker, was there with his wife, Susan. He looked sharply dressed in a tailored Lord and Taylor black trench coat with a red tartan wool scarf wrapped tightly around his neck. Sarah Martin, the local decorator, stood tall and stately against the old oak tree, glancing repeatedly at her watch, having arrived hurriedly at the last minute.

Father Luke Grayson, the Catholic priest, hatless and wearing his black suit and collar, stood in the midst of a group of elderly women, wearing an expression of what appeared to be slight dismay. Father Luke had a long neck, stiffly held, and he cocked his head upward in such a way that the casual observer would believe that he was looking down his nose at the "rental preacher."

As Pat's glance traveled around the crowd, over farmers and professors and even a few students, it stopped at the very back of the crowd on two men who seemed out of place. It wasn't that they looked that much different—they were two average-looking guys in black overcoats and sunglasses. Like Pat, the men seemed to be watching the crowd. Suddenly, one glanced at Pat and held her gaze, looking at her straight in her eyes. She smiled slightly, feeling her face turning red, as he continued to look at her without expression. Embarrassed, she turned her attention back to the service as the minister intoned: "Into your hands, oh merciful Savior, we commend your servant Joe. Acknowledge, we humbly beseech you, a sheep of your own fold, a lamb of your own flock, a sinner of your own redeeming. Receive him into the arms of your mercy, into the blessed rest of everlasting peace, and into the glorious company of the saints in light. Amen."

Babe sighed heavily and Anastasia leaned over and put her

arms around her.

The pastor continued. "As God has called our brother from this life, we commit his body to the earth from which it was made. Ashes to ashes, dust to dust."

Deb stood huddled beside her friend. *Who ever thought of those words? What kind of comfort are they to a family?* she wondered.

Deb's glance settled on the big lake down the hill in the distance, and she realized at that moment that she had loved Ashland almost from the minute she had set foot in it. There was something about the lake—actually, a lot of her love of Ashland had to do with the lake. She felt such a connection, knowing that every day when she looked down the street, she would see that deep water. But Deb also loved Ashland for the community. Funny—she had lived in a small town before but it had been nothing like this. When she and Marc were first married, they'd moved to rural Ohio for ten years. She should have liked it. After all, she finished her law degree there, Marc started his first private practice there, their two oldest kids graduated from high school there, and Deb had given birth to their two youngest kids. They'd even tried rehabbing that blasted 150-year-old brick monstrosity. Despite all that, she had never been able to put down roots. *I never felt the connection like I do in this town.*

As the service droned on, Deb let her mind wander away from the service, instead settling on her first month here....

Within weeks of her arriving in Ashland, the mayor called Deb to ask her to be on the Ashland Park Commission. And then there were the tai chi classes down the street at the Chequamegon Court Club, and the Big Top Show under the big blue tent in summers. Liberally mix in the hospitality of the neighborhood; the ice cream truck and the Fourth of July block party, and even the silly Santa parade in the winter, and the result was a place that was hopelessly nostalgic and "small town" to most city folks, but Deb realized it was all part of Ashland's real secret.

This place—with its sometimes rough exterior but rich

history—had one important thing going for it. Anyone who cared to look could find a place here and be nourished by the nature and people who were hardy enough to live here——God knew it seemed a forbidding place for most Southerners.

Deb smiled, remembering that "Southerners" was what the people on the bay called everyone who lived south of the town.

It's remote and isolated and the winters are long and bitter cold, Deb thought. *But when the sun shines here, it's more glorious than any place I can remember. That's probably why Joe chose this place—a place where he could fit in and be accepted, even if he was a little crazy. Joe,* she thought, as she turned once more to the service, *you were a part of us, and you will be missed.*

"Please join me in our Lord's Prayer, and remember that everyone is invited for a lunch and a time to share stories at the Black Cat," continued the pastor. "Our Father, who art in heaven …"

Pat joined in on the timeless prayer and lost herself in the words she had said so many times before.

After the gun salute, people put flowers on the casket and then hurried to get warm in their cars; Pat, too, went forward, where she whispered her own prayer: "Joe, it was too early for you. I don't know what you were into, you crazy fool, but I'm sorry you left the parade before the last float went by. I didn't know you well—I don't think many did—but know this: you will be missed." She patted his casket. And Deb, standing beside her, dropped her rose, too.

Pulling her coat closer as they walked out of the little cemetery, Pat craned her neck, trying to see the two guys in the black suits, but they had disappeared.

"What are you looking at?" Deb asked, her voice muffled behind the thick scarf she had wrapped around her mouth.

"Trying to find those two guys who stood in the back."

"What two guys?" Deb asked distractedly as she greeted people along the way to the car.

"*What* two guys?" Pat echoed. "The two black suits who stood apart from everyone else. You must have seen them. Maybe they came with the army guys, but I don't think so because they would have been in uniform. If this were a movie, I'd think they were FBI or CIA."

"Pat!" Deb chided, stopping in the middle of the path. "Weren't you paying attention to the service at all?"

"I've done that service hundreds of times, I know what he said," Pat said guiltily, walking on. "But what do you really think? Remember how Joe always talked about calling the CIA over this or that?" Without waiting for Deb to answer, Pat continued. "I think they just might have been CIA. Do you know, one of them caught me watching them and stared me down! It gave me the chills."

"It's thirty degrees outside and the wind is blowing like crazy. Of course you have the chills!" Deb was starting to get a little irritated with Pat. "Come on; if you had been listening, you would know that lunch is being served at the Black Cat. Any luck and they'll be serving something hot with brandy in it, in honor of Joe."

They got into Pat's old Volvo, turned on the seat warmers, and followed the line of cars into town. There were so many people attending the lunch that the only parking space Pat could find was two blocks away from the coffeehouse.

"We could have just as well parked at home," Deb grumbled as they started walking the two blocks to the Black Cat.

"You have lived in a small town too long," Pat said, laughing. "This seems like parking close to me."

The place was already crowded and getting steamy, too, by the time Deb and Pat arrived. Anastasia and Helga stood with their brother close to the door, greeting people and shivering as the cold blew in.

Anastasia reached warmly for their hands as Deb and Pat approached her. "I am so glad you could make it," she told them. Turning to her brother, she said, "Spisibo—Jacob—you know Deb, yah? ? And this is her friend Pat. She is the other one that rescued us on Monday."

"Good to see you again, Deb. Thanks for helping us out. And Pat, thanks again for connecting the girls to us," Jacob responded, his face etched with exhaustion and grief.

Even in his grief-stricken state, Pat was struck with how much he resembled his brother, Joe; especially the identical brown eyes with the hint of a twinkle. She looked at Deb with a quick question

46

in her eyes as they moved on to let someone else talk to the family and to find a table where they could sit.

"Don't look at me that way," Deb responded, without waiting for Pat to ask. "I was going to tell you. I just haven't had a chance. Alice and Anastasia came in to meet with me about probating Joe's estate. Actually, it's quite interesting. And I can't wait to tell you about it because it's going to be in the paper some time this week."

"In the paper? Come on, spill the beans. I want to hear it all."

"Not here. Nobody knows yet. Besides, I want to get some of those yummy bread things before they're gone. Come on."

Deb walked up to the counter that was laden with steaming pots of white vegetarian chili, beer-cheese soup, thick slices of sourdough bread, and big urns of hot cider and hot chocolate, served buffet style. Pat followed her, complaining, "That's not fair."

But Deb just smiled and reached for some hot cider. A few of the regulars made room for them at the large front table. Pat looked around for the hot toddies.

Chapter Nine

PAT WOKE UP THE FOLLOWING MORNING TO DEFUSED SILENCE, THE KIND OF SILENCE that can only come about only when there is snow. Tossing back her blankets, she jumped out of bed and ran to the window in her big old newly purchased Victorian home. She looked out at a scene that only could be called a winter wonderland. Snow was on the trees and on the rooftops, and it was accumulating quickly on the street that was already in need of plowing. And it was still snowing. Deb had assured Pat that once it started snowing, because Ashland was right on Lake Superior, there would soon be a "lake effect," which meant they could expect more snow than regions that were not situated next to the lake.

The snow was so white, it was blinding. "Yippee!" Pat gave a little dance.

"What now?" Mitchell grumbled. "First you do your yoga in bed at 5:30, and yes, before you ask, of course it wakes me up, and then you're dancing around like a kid, and it's what?" He squinted at the clock. "Not even seven? What happened to the 'relaxing time' up north?"

Pat went back to the bed and kissed Mitchell on the cheek. "Oh, you old bear. I do the yoga in bed because it's softer than the floor, and you want me to be healthy, don't you? But the dance—that was the first-snow-of-the-year dance. Come see. It must have snowed six inches already."

Mitchell groaned and pulled the pillow over his head.

Pat stepped into her slippers and Mitchell's old robe and then hurried downstairs——she was meeting Deb at eight for coffee. There had been so many people at the lunch yesterday; Deb hadn't had the chance to tell her what happened with Joe's family. The only thing Deb did tell Pat was that they were having guests for coffee at 8:30, so she had better be on time if she wanted to hear the news before they got there. Pat walked out into the mud room, looking for her boots as her oatmeal warmed in the microwave.

Deb walked her prancing golden retriever on his dailies around Chapple Avenue, then quickly dropped him off at home, leaving the pooper-scooper outside. She was eager to get to the Black Cat to meet Pat.

Deb smiled at Sam, standing behind the counter, as she entered the coffeehouse. "Can you believe this snow?" she asked, tossing her coat on a chair and gathering up the paper to see if there was any mention of Joe's funeral. Taking the cup of Velvet Hammer that Sam offered, she looked around the coffeehouse at the assembled locals and waited for her chronically late friend.

As she sipped her brew, Deb marveled again that the gods must be with her this year. When she'd convinced Pat and Mitchell to move to Ashland it just so happened that there were several magnificent Victorians for sale within a three-block area of her house. In Ashland, as Deb so often told them, it was still possible to get a bargain on a great home. She'd never expected that she and Pat actually would live in the same town—their life choices and circumstances had drawn them in different directions. Now, she loved that she was living her fantasy of walking up the street for coffee or sitting on the porch together and solving the world's problems or having long discussions about the latest book they had read.

Deb was just finishing her first cup when Pat arrived. Deb smiled as Pat came in saying hi to folks as if she had lived here forever.

"What's going on? Is the yoga practice helping you learn to be on time?" Deb teased. Before Pat could respond, Deb, bursting with anticipation, blurted out, "Wait 'til I tell you what I learned yesterday! While you were talking to the neighbors at the memorial lunch, I was sitting with Jacob and his two sisters. They were regaling me with stories about Joe, and apparently, he *did* win the Minnesota state lottery about ten years ago. He didn't even pick the numbers—just let the machine do it. And get this: he won something like $200,000! After that, he traveled to Florida every winter, but it wasn't until a year ago that he wrote to his sisters, telling them that he would pay their way to come here and get established in a new life."

Pat nodded eagerly, encouraging Deb to continue. After taking a sip of her coffee, Deb went on. "They said that they thought he might have won a different lottery a second time, but they weren't sure about the details of that one. Joe would give little hints during his phone calls that he had come into some more money, but he would always say his phone was bugged, so he couldn't give details. So he never actually said how much money or how he came by it, just that his own little lotteries had been very good to him. Can you believe his luck? What are the odds? And get this: Anastasia told me that her brother had been decorated with medals three different times for his bravery in Vietnam and that he thought Joe *did* do undercover work for the army during part of his stint there. And that," Deb finished, settling back in her chair, "is why the women asked to meet here at 8:30 this morning—they are the guests I mentioned. They seem to think we can help them find out what happened to Joe's money. Go figure. Also, they want us to help them look into what really caused his death." Deb sighed heavily. "I guess, being from Russia, they just don't trust the police to do a good job. What do you think of that?"

"I'm speechless," Pat said honestly. "Here we've joked about writing a mystery, but instead we're getting involved in one." Grabbing another cup of coffee, Pat started pulling up a few more chairs.

She never could have guessed that within a few weeks, they would be on a plane to the West Indies, having gotten involved up to their proverbial necks.

Later that day, Detective Gary LeSeur's office phone rang, startling him from his revelry—he'd been thinking about his upcoming ski vacation to Lyons, France, with ten of his friends, all of whom made an annual wifeless pilgrimage to a European ski slope each January.

"Hi, Gary," he heard the voice on the other end of the line greet him. "It's Ruth Epstein. Just wanted to give you a head's up. I got the preliminary toxicology results back from the autopsy on Joe Abramov. Looks like it wasn't accidental. The pathologist is sending the report by mail, but Joe apparently had a high level of a drug called fentanyl. Too bad—for Joe and for you. Looks like you have some work to do."

LeSeur let out a deep sigh, as he tried to decide whether he should put his skis back in the closet.

Chapter Ten

THE TWO RUSSIAN SISTERS CAME IN WITH A SWIRL OF WIND AND SNOW AROUND THEM, but they didn't seem to mind the cold. Their entrance didn't seem to warrant the locals' stares anymore. In fact, a few who had been at the memorial service raised a hand in a friendly wave, and then went back to the politics of the day.

"Hi," Deb said as she made more room at the table. "How are you sleeping? I know this is a hard time for you."

"Yes, but I sleep well here," replied Anastasia, as she took off her coat.

"Will you be returning to Russia?" Pat asked.

Anastasia nodded. "Quite honestly, ve must. Joe had sent us the money to come, but ve really have no money to go back. And besides, it is all so confusing. That is vhy ve asked you to meet us today. Ve just can't figure out vhat happened to the money."

"Money?" Pat asked.

"Yes, I just don't understand it," Helga said. "Joe sent for us so that ve could start new life. He had many plans, but how could he make plans if there vas no money left from the lottery?"

"Ten years is a long time in which to spend a lot of money," Pat replied helpfully. "And the way he lived here—from what we saw—Joe didn't seem to have any left to spend."

"Oh, Joe told us that he lived very simply so no one vould know about his money. He vas afraid someone vould steal from him." Helga set down the roll that Deb had offered to her and wiped her fingers. "But that's not the money I am talking about. I'm referring to talking about money from second lottery." She looked at Deb and Pat expectantly.

Before either woman could respond, a portly man in an expensive suit approached their table. His smile was wide, but Pat thought it seemed a little shifty.

Ignoring Deb and Pat as if they weren't there, the man turned toward the Russians. "Ladies, you don't know me, but I hope I can be of help to you. I like to think of my family as the caretakers of this little hamlet. We've been here for generations. My name is Mike—Michael Williamson. Perhaps you could come into my office some time today. There are routine papers to go over whenever someone dies."

The sisters looked confused.

"At the bank, I mean," Williamson explained. "I'm the president of Great Northern, the local bank. So if you could just stop in …"

"Excuse me, but did Joe Abramov have an account with you?" Pat asked.

As if she was an annoyance, he pursed his lips in a half-smile. "Now that would be confidential information, wouldn't it?" he replied, somewhat arrogantly. Turning back to Anastasia, he continued. "Just stop in, if you would, today." Tipping his hat, Williamson walked confidently up to the counter to pick up his to-go cup.

Pat looked at the sisters. "Do you know for sure that there was a second lottery?"

"Well, he vas secretive," Anastasia answered. "You know how he vas, but he assured us he had von again. 'A big one this time,' he said. And that's vhy he could send for us and assure us all of new life here. But now our brother Jacob tells us there are no lotteries von recently, so ve do not understand. Vhat could he have been saying?"

"Maybe he was just delusional," Pat blurted out.

"Pat," Deb said, frowning.

"No, no—I know you think he strange, and he vas," Anastasia agreed. "From the var, I mean. He always thought someone or some group vas after him. He send us money to get here. And money for clothes to travel. He made very specific plans for us, so I believed him. But if there vere no lotteries in Wisconsin or Minnesota von lately, could there have been one in another state? Ve vere hoping

54

you vould help."

"Well, it would be easy enough to check in other states, but if a big one had been won, we would have heard of it by now, and his name would probably have been announced," Deb said. "Do you think he meant he came by the money another way?"

The sisters looked at each other. Lowering her voice, Anastasia continued, "First, ve vould like you to help us find out if it vas lottery. Then, if not ...vell; in his letter he didn't exactly say it vas lottery. Here, let me read it to you." She pulled a well-worn letter out of her pocket and glanced down the page. "Here ... here it is, after he invited us to come," she said. Anastasia began to read in Russian, translating as she went along.

Sis, finally I can send for you all. I just know you can have a better life here. Don't worry; I have enclosed the money for all of you to come and some for clothes to travel, but there is more—much more. I have recently come into another lottery, you could call it. And my wish is to share it with you. I can't wait until you get here, and we can start our new life together. Things are going to be different from now on. Why, if we want to, we can even buy that island I always dreamed about. And no one will be able to get to me again. I know this may sound crazy, but it's true. My ship has come in, and I want you to be aboard. See you at the airport.

Your loving brother, *Joe*

"What" Pat asked with her eyes, as she looked up at Deb to see if she had finished reading it. Before Deb could respond Sarah, the town decorator and owner of Design Outlet, arrived. Sarah carried a large bag of samples that she set down on the table with a grunt of relief.

"Here are the samples you asked for."

"Thanks," Pat replied. "That was very thoughtful. You didn't have to bring those here. I'd have come to your shop and picked them up." Indicating the others, she asked Sarah, "Have you met the Abramov sisters?" She put the samples on the floor by her chair. "Of course, you met yesterday. My, what a busy table we are sitting at," Pat observed. "Mike Williamson just stopped by, too."

As Sarah nodded in greeting, she grabbed her daily coffee fix from the barista's outstretched hand and smiled, in exchange handed him two dollars. She then turned to Pat. "Mikey? Came over special, did he?" Sarah's round eyes were wide with interest, her eyebrows raised. "I suppose he would."

Pat stirred her coffee. "He said he represents the community, his family having been in this town for generations."

Sarah smirked. "He usually says centurios—since the pilgrims, the way *he* tells it. Of course, it's really only been three or four generations."

"Wow, the way people move these days, that's actually impressive."

"Oh, it impresses *him*, all right." Sarah sipped her double espresso, wrinkling her nose as if it had a bad smell, then quickly concealed it. "He hasn't lived here all his life. He got out before the ink was dry on his high school diploma. Actually came back to town to take over the bank after his father had his heart attack." She turned to the sisters with an expression of apology. "Sorry, didn't mean to bring in town gossip. Actually, he used to come into the Black Cat about once a week and play chess with your brother and buy him a coffee. Joe always got him to put brandy in his. So I guess he can't be all bad, although you couldn't prove it by me." Sarah swallowed the last drop from her small cup and then set it on the table. "You know, it's strange," Sarah said, "but this is the first time Mike has been in here for about six months. He and Joe seemed to stop playing chess all of a sudden, and it was like Mike was avoiding Joe after that. I never heard why." Sarah put on her coat and wrapped her scarf around her neck and added, "Not that it was any of my concern. You know Joe—he could keep a secret better than anyone."

"What do you think they argued about?" Deb asked. "Six months is a long time for an argument to last."

Sarah shook her head, although bundled as she was in her winter wear, the movement was almost imperceptible. Suddenly she remembered that her truck was still running and got up to leave. "I didn't actually say they argued. I mean, I didn't see it or anything, but it was strange that their games stopped." Turning to the sisters, she added one final thought. "Joe was a good man; he forgave anyone anything, ordinarily. He stopped regularly in my shop, ladies, and sometimes helped out with moving heavy carpet and odd jobs. I liked him. I'll miss him. You need anything, come see me."

Putting on her gloves, she turned and walked out the door.

"Well," said Deb, getting up, "I'm sorry, but I need to get to court. I don't know if there really is a way we can help you, but if there is, you can count on me. Why don't you talk to the banker this afternoon? You said you're having dinner with Jacob tonight. See if he has any ideas, and then ..." She glanced at Pat for confirmation. . "Meet us here tomorrow morning at eight. Does that sound all right? I'm still not sure what we can do. Frankly, it's just a shot in the dark that we will ever find out what really happened to the money. Oh, and be careful with the banker. You heard what Sarah said. It could be she's just mad because he turned her down for a business loan last winter, but I don't know him well, so be careful."

"Thank you so much, yes, ve vill meet with the banker, and ve vill be careful," Anastasia responded.

"So it is agreed we will meet tomorrow at eight."

After the others left, Pat settled herself comfortably at the table and had a second cup of the French roast as she read the daily newspaper. But though her eyes were scanning the headlines, her mind was elsewhere. *What happened to Joe's money?*

Back in her office after Court, Deb's intercom beeped twice on her desk, startling her and interrupting her thoughts as she sorted through the daily pile of mail. She picked up the phone and Kris, her secretary, informed Deb that Jacob Abramov was on line one. "He wants to make an appointment to meet with you about probating his brother's estate."

"Go ahead and make an appointment," Deb replied, a hint of anticipation in her voice. As she returned her attention to the pile of mail and sticky notes, Deb couldn't help wondering, *How deep into this family drama am I going to go, anyway? This goes so much deeper than typical probate work...so many family dramas.*

Deb sighed and sat back on her comfy new chair as Kris brought her a steaming cup of coffee. "Thanks," Deb said gratefully.

"How did you know I needed this?" She took a sip and sighed again. "And just the way I like it."

"It just seemed like a two-cup morning," Kris replied, smiling at her boss. "And besides, I've got that gorgeous detective on line two for you, and he didn't make one joke, so I'm assuming it's something serious." With that she saluted and quickly left, shutting the door behind her.

Deb gulped the steaming-hot Rain Forest Blend and picked up the phone. "Hi, Detective LeSeur, enough snow for you?" Deb started with the traditional opening of the North.

"Almost. Could use another few inches on the trails for my snowmobile, though. As if I'll have my machine out any time soon." With the amenities finished, he changed gears. "Deb ... I'm calling you about your clients, the Abramov sisters. Can I assume you are also representing the brother, Jacob?"

Deb sat up in her chair, no longer feeling so tired. "That's correct. Just on probate stuff." Then, risking his laughing at her, Deb continued. "Why? Should my clients be looking for a seasoned defense attorney?"

LeSeur hesitated momentarily, then said, "Actually, I need you to help me—that is, the department—with something."

"As long as it doesn't interfere with client/attorney confidentiality," Deb answered cautiously. "Don't ask me something I can't do, but otherwise, shoot."

"We got the preliminary autopsy reports." LeSeur cleared his throat. "Joe Abramov didn't die of natural causes."

Deb waited, and when the silence became pronounced, she asked, "You mean he killed himself or ...?"

"Truth is, it's looking a lot less like suicide and a lot more like murder. But I'm telling you this for a reason."

"Okay," Deb responded, all thoughts of her hot cuppa gone from her head, as she grabbed for pencil and notepad.

"I need to inform the family before it leaks out in the press, and as they are your clients ... well, I was hoping you could be there for the women when I do so. They aren't suspects—they weren't even here when he died—but this will be another blow for them.."

"Of course," Deb responded, "just tell me where and when."

"Best you come in to my office with them at, say, 1:00? Now, here are the ground rules." His tone became more serious. "Let me tell them. I won't be sharing specific details, and you should not be aggressive about details. If they ask questions, I'll try to answer them honestly. But I am asking you to be there to support them— that's all. Is that clear? Can I count on you?"

"Done and done," Deb responded. "I'll bring them in, but I'll leave the telling to you. And LeSeur, just one question, please?"

"Curiosity killed the cat, Deb," he responded. "But in this case, the cat was poisoned. Is that your question? See you at 1:00." And with a click the phone went dead.

"Kris," Deb called out to the reception area. "I really think it might be a three-cup day. Could you get the Abramov sisters on the phone?" Then as an afterthought, she shouted, "Are there any of those great cookies left out there?"

A nap hadn't been on Pat's agenda, but she dozed off over the latest mystery she had picked up at the Book Nook. The phone startled her out of a pleasant dream about beaches and cabana boys. By the third ring she had managed to find the right button and answered, a little louder than necessary, "Hello? Hello? Did I press the right button?"

A stifled laugh from Deb on the other end told her she had. "I just have a minute, but I just had to call, so listen and don't talk," Deb said hurriedly.

Pat bristled momentarily but then asked, "What?"

"I said *listen*," Deb repeated. "In half an hour I'm taking the ladies to meet with 'Detective Hunk' about the autopsy report. Guess what? You won't believe it ... it really was murder. Poison, specifically. Gotta go. Say a prayer for me that I'll do the right things when the sisters learn of this." And without waiting for an answer Deb hung up, leaving Pat with her mouth open, looking quizzically at the phone.

Chapter Eleven

As Pat glanced at the calendar in the kitchen, she chided herself. *I really am going to have to get to making Christmas cookies soon.* Wiping off the crumbs on the counter from lunch, she hedged. *But it doesn't really have to be today. Of course, it can't be tomorrow because we're meeting the sisters, and then we might be going down to the Cities for the weekend.*

She was still thinking about it with distaste when the door bell rang. The god awful one at the back door that played *God Bless America. Someone's come to visit us in our new house,* she thought. And throwing the dish rag into the sink and smiling, she went through the hall to answer it.

The man standing at Pat's back door seemed buried in his jacket, hat, and scarf—he was so completely covered that Pat didn't recognize him.

"Yes?" she asked tentatively. "Can I help you?"

"Pat, it's me, Bill Montgomery from the Black Cat," he said, taking off his scarf so she could see his face. "I thought I might be able to help you. I knew Joe as well or better than anyone in town, and I know this town well, too."

Pat looked confused. "I'm sorry, Bill ... help me in what way?"

Bill stamped his feet and blew on his mittened hands. "I imagine many people are willing to help you and Deb all they can for poor Joe's sisters' sake, but you might not know who they are. So I thought I would just stop by for a chat." He stamped his feet again and tugged his hat farther over his ears. "Can I come in?"

What am I doing? Pat thought. "Of course, Bill," she said, opening the door and drawing him inside. "You must be freezing."

Once the door closed behind him, Bill shook the snow off his boots and hat. Pat took his coat and hat and hung them up in the mud room before leading Bill into the kitchen. The room was warm and cozy, just right for a chat, and she put on the tea kettle. Bill settled himself at Pat's kitchen table as if he had been there many times before.

"Did you know Liz Case, the woman who lived here before?" Pat asked as she got the cups and some cookies from the cupboard. "Oh, yes, we were good friends, Liz and I," Bill replied. "She bought some photos from me and helped me quite a lot. She talked me up to her society friends, and they bought drawings and photos, too. Too bad she split up with her husband and moved away. She was a lot of fun." Settling more comfortably in his chair, he continued, "But I came to help you with your search for Joe's killer."

"Killer?" Pat repeated curiously. "Why would you think Joe was murdered?"

"Joe was a good guy, you know," Bill went on, as if he had his own agenda. "Kind and certainly trustworthy. He knew secrets all around town. All the little things he saw and never said a word about. We used to make dinner together a couple of times a week. You didn't know that, did you?" Bill reached out for the hot cup that Pat had set in front of him.

Pat would not be deterred. "The coroner's report hasn't come out yet, as far as I know. And who told you Deb and I are helping the sisters? Frankly, we haven't even decided there is anything we can do to help them. Although for Joe's sake, I suppose we will try." She put the cookies on a beautiful plate. *That always makes them taste better*, she thought as she brought them to the table.

"Thanks. I guess I just assumed that you two were helping them. After all, everyone knows Deb is helping them with his estate, whatever there is. As for murder, don't you think he died rather strangely?" Putting the cookie down, Bill backtracked. "I really was just speculating about his being killed."

"What I guess I really would like to know," Pat said thoughtfully, "is who might have taken advantage of Joe." She gave him a reassuring smile. "I don't mean you, obviously, but who?"

"You know that he won that lottery ten years ago, right?" Bill replied. Seeing her startled look, he said, "Sure, I know all about that. Joe told me long ago. He was naive in some ways, and I'm afraid people took advantage of that."

Then they put their heads together, trying to think of different people in town who might have been in a position to borrow money from Joe.

"Well, let's see," Bill said, as he poured them each another cup of tea. "The good thing about a small town is everyone knows everyone else's troubles. The bad thing is everyone thinks they know each other's troubles, but that's not always true. For example, there's Mike Williamson."

"Oh, yes," Pat agreed. "I met him today. He's the banker, right?"

"Yup, a local boy who has taken over Great Northern Bank, the only privately owned bank here in Ashland. Took it over from his father. Now Mike is the third generation of Williamsons to try his hand at the banking business. His grandfather, Sam, was well respected in the community for his willingness to help his patrons. With Sam, a person could get a loan with a promise and a handshake. None of the elaborate appraisals, long financial forms, committee meetings, and crazy loan fees. Yes, those were certainly the good old days. Sam was a good judge of character and knew everyone. He inspired trust and confidence, you know what I mean? People felt good handing over their money to him for safekeeping."

Bill continued regaling her with his knowledge of local history. "Now, his son, Mike's father, Charlie, just wasn't cut from the same cloth and didn't seem to have the same people skills as Sam. Like anyone who has to follow in the footsteps of a founder of a successful enterprise, Charlie just never was able to fill his dad's shoes. And he could only go so far on his father's name and reputation. People in town soon discovered he lacked the interest and know-how that inspired trust in a banker. He cared more about his golf game than the bank. In time, a lot of people took their banking to the new S&L down the street, even though it wasn't locally owned and operated. Like the old saw says, familiarity breeds contempt."

"This is very interesting," Pat said. "But what does it have to do with Joe and Mike?"

"I'm getting there, I'm getting there," Bill assured her. "I just

63

wanted you to understand what Mike walked into. When Mike took over the family business eight years ago, he had been gone a long time. After graduating from UW Madison with an MBA, he went to the Twin Cities to work. He always thought he would make it big, but I don't think that really happened. He was already middle-aged and graying when he was called home to save the bank. Mike was thrust into the position as bank president out of a combination of family loyalty and duty. Charlie, the bank president, had been forced out by the board of directors after he was committed to the local detox unit for the third time in three years. Even in a small town, you can only look the other way so many times before being confronted with the miserable reality of a failing bank. I might even feel sorry for Mike if he wasn't such a horse's rear end most of the time. That guy is so full of himself, you would think one day he will just explode."

"So how did he save the bank?" Pat asked.

"It looked for a time as though the bank couldn't survive. Reports and records were in disarray, and the state audit disclosed negligence and questionable loan practices. It seems old Charlie wasn't beneath giving loans to his golf buddies, for whatever they wanted. Mike is a hybrid of his father and grandfather. He came in determined to save the family name and reputation, come hell or high water. Whoo-ee, he hired all new workers, gave the bank a facelift, and began taking an active role in the community. You ask me, he is a busybody, with an inflated sense of his own importance. You know the kind. Someone who likes to put his two cents in by serving on lots of civic committees and who believes his ideas for the community are better than everyone else's. I've got to admit, in the last few years it seems as if the bank has been doing better. It's almost like Mike had a magic wand. No one is quite sure how it happened, but each year for the past five, the amounts of deposits in the bank have shown a dramatic increase. My question is: how or where did he get the cash he needed to keep that place going until it turned around?"

"Doesn't sound like you like him much."

"I don't, and that's the truth. I needed money a few years back. I had a show coming up and needed just a small loan to tide me over. He acted like he was affronted by me asking. 'I'm not my grandfather or my dad,' he said to me. 'If you need the money, get a job like the rest of us.' No, I don't like him one bit," Bill said firmly, taking another bite of his cookie.

"So why is this related to Joe?" Pat asked.

"Joe had money. And he had it in that bank. I know for a fact he didn't trust leaving his money there. He had some trouble a while back, because he realized the interest wasn't being put in his account. If you're having trouble in a bank, I would think having a few hundred thousand to play around with might be helpful."

"Anyone else you think might have needed money?" Seeing Bill look at the empty cookie plate, Pat hurried to fill it again. *Cookies are little enough payment for the local scoop,* she thought.

"Next," Bill said, counting off on his fingers, "that would be Sarah Martin. Sarah moved here twenty-eight years ago with her first husband and settled on Chapple to raise her children. She quickly became an outspoken and involved community leader, even as she went through two more husbands. She has great taste in decorating. I wish I could afford to hire her to come and do my apartment. Her taste in men is dubious at best. Man, how that woman can pick 'em!"

Pat leaned forward with great interest. Encouraged by Pat's eager anticipation, Bill continued. "Driven by frenetic energy, she opened a decorating business on Main Street and quickly gained a reputation as a fashionable designer who knew the insides of nearly everyone's home. Yet at the same time, she had trouble finding her way around her own office. And being in all the best houses, she knew more secrets, like whose husband was sleeping with whom or what business was about to go under. If there is a new building project going on in the county, you can bet that Sarah is somewhere in the middle of it." Bill obviously relished his role as gossip monger. "Now here's the good part: Sarah's third husband, Jack, had joined her in the business in the role of helping out, whatever that means. In his case, it was mostly going fishing. At least that was how he explained his increasingly frequent absences from the store. But Jack was out fishing for more than trout, if you know what I mean. When she found him in their bed with a young chippie from the college, she ended up paying him an inflated sum in order to be rid of him. Everyone thought Sarah's decorating business would be unable to survive after that. But my question is, even with laying off most of her employees and working twelve hours a day, how does she, out of the blue, purchase the big empty storefront across the street from her dinky store? Somehow, she managed to completely refurbish it, rent out the empty spaces, and even acquire several other rental properties. How did she do that?"

"Maybe she had finally got herself a sugar daddy," Pat suggested.

"The way she picks them?" he snorted. "No, but she *was* friends with Joe."

Pat shifted uncomfortably in her seat. "I like Sarah," Pat confessed. "She's a good neighbor. But it's true that decorating stores aren't known for making the most money. I wonder where she got the money." She shifted uncomfortably. "Isn't there someone else with motive to kill Joe? Some other reason?" she asked.

"Only one I can think of off hand," Bill said, grinning. "But you're not going to like it, you being a pastor and all."

"What do you mean?"

"Our local Catholic priest."

"You've got to be kidding!"

"Nope, I'm serious. Father Luke is one of the fortunate few who never seems to age. Middle-aged, but he still looks like he's in his early twenties. Unfortunately, his looks do not coincide with his personality. Have you made it over to his church yet?"

Pat shook her head.

"Well, he's very pious, always quoting his bishop—the bishop says this, the bishop says that. He wears one of those Tupperware white plastic collars—you know what I mean? You never see him without it. I mean, it's like an advertising billboard saying 'I'm a priest; make way.' Some of us even wonder whether he sleeps in it. He works hard, but his congregation is so old, I don't even know how they keep the doors open. But do you want to know what's strange? They recently embarked on a half-million-dollar face lift to the building. And he used to visit with Joe all the time. It wouldn't be the first time a church has bilked a poor sucker out of his money."

Pat blushed. She knew that it was true that there were some dishonest pastors and priests out there. But there were so many who were just trying hard to be of help. Standing, Pat smiled. "Thank you," she said sincerely as she showed him to the door. "You have been very helpful, and thank you for being a friend to Joe."

As she closed the door behind Bill, she turned and walked to the phone to call Deb at her office. Glancing at the plate of cookies, Pat noticed that Bill had eaten them all. Postponing the call for later, she decided to drive to Gabriele's German Cookies and Chocolate shop on Main Street. *If people are going to be dropping in, I'd better stock up*, she thought.

Later that evening, Anastasia welcomed Deb and Pat into the hotel room. "Thank you very much for coming," she said. "I hope you'll understand my reasons for calling you so soon." She gave them both a big hug.

"Don't mention it," said Deb. "The truth is, if you hadn't called, I would have phoned you." Taking their coats and placing them on the bed, Anastasia gestured to the two other chairs in the room.

"It's leaked out to the papers--the suspicious circumstances about Joe's death," Deb explained. "I thought we should talk"

"Leaked? Oh, I see. Someone gave information, you mean. Yes, news reporters have called and asked for interviews. I just can't understand it."

"Now, dear, it's to be expected, but as your attorney, I'd advise you to say you have no comment at this time. You don't have to discuss it with anyone."

"Yah, ve even had a call from some magazine vanting to do an article! Vat next? A book?" Anastasia threw up her hands. "Also, the officer who vas in charge of investigation called and vants to talk to my sister and me." Wringing her hands, Anastasia started pacing. "Said he is cooperation with the CIA! I can't believe our brother could have been a spy or something!"

"Calm down and sit," Pat said soothingly. "There's just not enough room in here to pace. I'm afraid there had to be some cooperation with the CIA and the army. But I can't really believe it had to do with his past. How could they hope to find any evidence after all this time has passed? And anything people from that time might have known surely has been tarnished by the passage of time. Too bad, but it can't be helped. Don't worry so much. This is America, not the old USSR. Anyway, it's just procedure."

"Yes," Deb chimed in. "Detective LeSeur is a good man. You can trust him."

"Maybe it's all a mistake," Anastasia said, starting to weep. "Maybe the laboratory reports were wrong."

Deb caught Pat's eye. "Maybe," she allowed, "but I wouldn't count on it."

Deb took one last bite of the spicy chicken stir-fry with mushrooms that she so loved and then put down her fork. She and Marc were just finishing dinner alone—Eric was at soccer practice—in the cozy kitchen of their hundred-year-old Victorian home. She sighed contentedly as she looked across the table at her "personal chef." *I am so lucky*, she thought, *with a husband who likes to cook, who insists on it, even after a long day at the office. What more could a woman want?*

Marc opened up the newspaper and settled back in his chair. "I heard at work today that they think the dead guy down the street was murdered."

"I've had my suspicion about that for a while, but I haven't said anything because it sounds so far-fetched," Deb replied hesitantly. "Pat and I are pretty close to this whole thing, what with going to the Black Cat every morning and knowing Joe and all."

"You women aren't sticking your noses where they don't belong, are you?" Marc demanded. "After all, you aren't trained as investigators. You don't know anything about this stuff. And besides, if it was a murder, it's too dangerous for you to have anything to do with it. This is a small town, and you could open yourselves up as targets for the real killer. I think you'd better just leave the investigating to the professionals."

Deb sighed, suppressing her rebellious instincts. *There he goes again*, she thought. *I just want to help some people, but there's my honey to add a dose of realism to make me think twice.*

Part of her agreed with Marc, and she liked that he tempered her often reckless enthusiasm, but other times, she felt like a rebellious teenager. *Is this going to be one of those times when I reject his well-intentioned advice?* she thought.

Deb paused before saying, "You don't give Pat and me enough credit. We are intelligent, insightful women, after all. Do you think I'm really going to intentionally put myself in danger? Besides, we have a lot of threads of information, and I am very good at connecting the dots. If I have something to offer to help this situation, why not use it?"

Marc rolled his eyes. "You're going to do what you want anyway, aren't you?" he asked resignedly. He smiled affectionately at Deb and added, "I just want you to be careful."

Chapter Twelve

There was a sharp drop in the temperature that night, and once again there was light snow by the next morning.

"Put on your long underwear," Mitchell called as Pat dressed.

She put on her winter boots, a thick wool scarf, her long gray wool coat, black gloves, and a furry hat. *I am ready*, she thought as she looked at herself in the front hall mirror before opening the front door onto Chapple Avenue.

Even warmly dressed, Pat was unprepared for the arctic blast that met her as she stepped outside—the wind hit like icicles. She put on her sunglasses to shield her eyes from the glare and the wind, but tears had already formed in the corners of her eyes. The outdoor sounds seemed muffled by the snowfall so that the only thing she heard was the crunching of her boots against the snow.

Deb was just coming out of her house as Pat arrived. Deb turned back to toss a biscuit to Strider, her golden retriever, and then pulled the door shut behind her. The two friends braced themselves against the bitter wind off the lake as they walked the five blocks to the Black Cat at much brisker pace than usual. The usual crowd of middle-aged men was sitting at the front table in the coffeehouse, loudly talking politics and ranting about the latest government act of malfeasance. Offering the women a quick smile as they passed, Bill Montgomery continued his conversation, his voice filled with indignation. "And I don't care what they say, this president is a criminal, and he should be tried in a court of law, just like any other."

Deb and Pat approached the counter and greeted Kait, who offered them Italian blend—a little spice against the cold, she'd said.

They decided to sit in the back room to talk, where they wouldn't be distracted by the lively conversation in the main room. "It's great fun to live in a town where politics and issues are constantly being discussed," Deb said to Pat, "but right now we've got more important things to talk about. Besides, since the Russians are meeting us, we don't need the details of what they are doing blabbed all over town by lunch."

They had just settled in and were warming their hands on their cups, when their Russian friends arrived.

"The man out front said you were back here," Anastasia began.

Deb smiled in greeting, noting that the women looked tired— their shoulders were bent and there were new lines on their faces.

They both took off their gloves and sat down, as Anastasia said, "Ve vent to the bank for our appointment vith the banker to try to find out if Joe's money is there. Dat Mr. Williamson vas not helpful. He vas polite, yah, but vague about his dealings with Joe in the past."

"He vould not tell us if Joe had money in an account," Helga put in.

Anastasia nodded. "He said ve vould have to vait until probate papers come through before ve can get details from bank. He said Joe vas his friend, but if this vere true, vhy vouldn't he help Joe's sisters?" She shook her head, clearly confused. "Ve think Joe did have money. Our brother Jacob thinks someone in this town may have taken it."

Deb patted Anastasia's hand reassuringly. "Pat and I will help you find out about Joe's money, if we can," she said kindly, "but we'll need to have a lot more information if we are going to help."

"Ask anything," Anastasia said eagerly. "Our lives are open to you."

"Well ..." Pat began thoughtfully, "this may seem obvious, but did you look around Joe's apartment?"

Anastasia shook here her head. "To tell you truth, ve only vent in to find clothes for his funeral." Looking at her sister, she went on. "Ve vere hoping you vould go over there vith us."

Gulping down the rest of her cup, Pat looked at Deb. "Have you got the time, Deb?'

Picking up her cell, Deb began to dial. "I don't have to go to the office for appointments today. Let me just call Kris, and then we might as well go now."

Putting on their coats and all the required accessories of a northern winter, they started across the street. Their breath made billows of white clouds as they stepped out into the cold air. The wind was blowing so hard that they had to push against it to make headway. The Russian women, on the other hand, were like sailboats in a strong gale—they just seemed to point their bows into the wind and go.

The building was a brick three-story that was divided into six apartments. Joe's, as indicated on the antiquated mailboxes inside the door, was upstairs in the back. Pat sniffed the air—the hall smelled of age and cleaning fluids. Mariachi music was drifting quietly out of a first-floor flat.

They clomped up the wooden stairs in their winter boots. Pat had to stop periodically to rest because she was so easily winded when climbing any stairs. She was glad there were only two stories.

. "Do you have the key?" Deb asked Anastasia as they stood outside Joe's apartment waiting for Pat to arrive.

"Yah," Anastasia answered, opening the door. "You go first, please."

The room was dim; even though the shades were up, the weak December light streamed through dirty panes, and the room seemed bleak.

This is the place where Joe spent his last days, Pat thought. *How depressing.*

Deb hesitated before stepping over the threshold. "Are you sure we can be in here?" she asked.

"Yah. The detective said it vas all right"

Turning on the overhead light, Pat and Deb surveyed the tiny apartment: living room, small galley-type kitchen, two doors that probably led to the bathroom and bedroom.

"Nothing looks out of the ordinary," Deb commented.

"If anything," Pat added quietly, "it's extraordinary in its ordinariness." An old couch and chair with a reading lamp on a small table were all that filled the living room. The kitchen was surprisingly clean—one cup and plate in the sink, counters wiped, dish towel hung through the door handle of the fridge. Pat's eyes narrowed as she looked around again. "Did you come in and clean?" she asked.

"No, ve didn't," Anastasia answered. "I vas surprised to see that Joe kept his place so neat. As a boy, he vas messy, you know? Shoes here, shirt there." She smiled wistfully. "Our mother vould laugh to know that someone finally taught Joe not to drop his coat at the door.."

Helga smiled. "She does know, sister."

"Of course," Anastasia agreed quietly.

Pat felt a wave of despair. The sisters were counting on her and Deb to help. And yet, they didn't even know what they were looking for. What kind of clues did she expect to find—a lottery ticket behind, say, the picture frame on the wall? Or perhaps account numbers in the silverware drawer? *Oh, what the hell*, Pat thought. *If it was good enough for Agatha Christie ...* She walked over and pulled the picture from the wall. No luck. Darn!

"Let's look in the bedroom," Deb suggested.

The box spring and mattress were relatively new, although the nightstand seemed to be standard Salvation Army. Clothes were hung neatly in the closet; a pair of jeans were folded on the one chair in the corner. Against the wall was a computer desk with a sturdy chair next to it. And on the desk was a Dell computer that looked only a few years old.

"Have you tried getting into his files?" Deb asked, sitting down at the desk.

"My brother Jacob looked through them," Anastasia answered, "and said there vas nothing interesting."

Pat opened a closet door. "For a clean man, his closet is really dirty, she said. "Deb, why don't you check out the computer files while I look through this closet?" she suggested. "Anastasia, you and Helga could look in the bathroom. Remember, it might be just a scrap of paper or something written on a shelf." As soon as the sisters left the room, Pat whispered, "Deb, do you trust Jacob?"

"Well, I don't really know him, just from helping them with some papers, but he seems nice enough. Why? Do you think he found something on the computer?"

"I don't know; let's just hope he didn't delete anything. Let's not say anything to the sisters, though. After all, he is their brother. Start by seeing if there is a file called 'this is where I have all the money stashed,' and go from there."

Laughing, Deb settled into the chair. Finishing up in the closet, Pat looked at what she had collected: matchbooks from the bank, the Black Cat, and the local feed store, along with a scrap of paper that looked like some kind of shorthand:

Paint by number	24	10
Cash in hand	50	25
By design	10	10
Purgatory	28	5

Pat stared at it, getting a feeling that she should know what it was. *If these numbers across from the words ...*

She was brought out of her reverie by a call from the bathroom. "Pat, do you think this is anything?" Anastasia asked. She was holding an empty pill bottle with a label that read "fentanyl."

Pat turned the bottle over in her hand. "I don't recognize this drug," she said, almost to herself. "But why leave an empty bottle in the medicine cabinet?"

A knock at the door broke her concentration once again. Helga answered the door as Pat slipped the pill bottle into her pants pocket.

Helga smiled as she saw Bill standing at the door, holding a covered hot dish.

"Hello," he said. "Isn't this cold weather something? I just thought I would pop by and see if you were here. I brought a tuna hot dish, thinking if you were busy packing up stuff you might like to take a break." He walked in and headed for the kitchen, where he put the hot dish on the counter and then pulled out plates and forks from the cupboard. Pat smiled at the idea of how Midwestern it is that everyone brings food in times of tragedy whether it's needed or not.

"I guess I got used to having a meal over here with Joe, and I kind of miss it," said.

"You have been so helpful," Helga said, blushing a little as she looked at him.

"It vas so kind of you to bring this over. But please, let me take your coat and hat, and you sit. I vill serve your food."

"Bill has been so kind," said Anastasia to Pat as they came into the kitchen.

Bill smiled at Anastasia's comment. "Not at all, not at all. Joe was a friend, and I want to help his sisters, especially when they are as lovely as you two," Bill said, with a wink at Anastasia. "But I see you haven't gotten things bagged up yet for me to take to the Goodwill. Do you think you will do that today? I have time tonight to take the bags in."

Anastasia glanced at Pat. "Ve need to go through things first. Ve've been away from him for so long, you understand. But thank you."

"Well, just let me know, and I'll be glad to help," Bill responded amiably. "If you don't mind, I'll just go in and wash up for lunch."

Later, Pat and Deb bid good-bye to the sisters, and as they were leaving the apartment, Pat grumbled, "Can you believe this?"

"Believe what?" Deb asked.

"Believe that we couldn't find anything in there. I mean, detectives on TV and in books always seem to notice that clues just pop out at them." Pat sighed dejectedly. "What I'm worried about," she continued, "is that the sisters are counting on us for help, and we'll totally flop."

"I know what you mean," Deb agreed. "I suppose it's natural, not knowing anyone here, that they would lean on us. And I like them. But as detectives, we make a better pastor and lawyer. Still, we have to be missing something. Killers always make some stupid mistake. Let's each go over the apartment on our own and write down anything at all that seemed wrong."

"Agreed," Pat said, opening the door to bright sunshine. "Then if we don't find anything ... we'll just have to start letting them down easy." Deb smiled at her friend as they walked home.

Chapter Thirteen

"I HEARD YOU TWO HAVE BEEN MESSING AROUND WITH THE INVESTIGATION OF JOE'S death." Gary LeSeur stared accusingly at Pat and Deb, who were sitting comfortably in Deb's office.

"We are only helping his sisters," Deb insisted. "Anything we can tell them?"

Sighing heavily, LeSeur sat down next to Pat. "The fact is we have some suspects but no real evidence. Truth be told, unless it's someone from his past—and even that seems unlikely—and even if we think we know who did it, I'll probably never be able to do anything about it." He looked from one woman to the other. "Don't look so disgruntled, ladies. We'll keep trying. Our leads aren't helping. You know how it is; everyone is afraid. Unfortunately, they might be covering something that would help us solve this thing and not even realize it." Scratching his head, he leaned back in his chair.

"And of course, I have to wonder if one of them knows who the killer is. People are so stupid sometimes. They think they can't possibly be in danger if they just keep quiet. But it only takes one slip, and if the killer feels threatened ... well, he or she has killed before."

"Of course people are worried and scared," Deb said thoughtfully. "And maybe one of them does know something and is good at acting. But my guess is no one knows anything for sure, and that's why they're so skittish."

"But look at it from their points of view," LeSeur continued.

"You couldn't help wondering, could you? Going over and over the bits and pieces of possible information, and trying to remember, trying to piece together. 'Course, that's my job—rounding up all the pieces and putting them together if I can." Gary chuckled as he stood up, indicating their chat had ended. "We'll do our best. You two stay out of it, and if, in the end, we have no evidence, then that's what we'll have to accept. Who knows? Maybe we'll get lucky."

Deb narrowed her eyes as she studied LeSeur. "I know you," she said. "You don't believe it will ever be solved, do you?"

He looked at them and shaking his head, he walked out of Deb's office.

Pat and Deb stared after him, wondering if his shaking his head was supposed to indicate that he was exasperated with them ... or if it was an acknowledgement that he didn't think he'd solve the case.

"So much for his help," Pat snorted. "But you were saying you think you missed something. What was it?"

"If I knew, it wouldn't be missing," Deb retorted. "I've been going over it in my mind, again and again, and I can't place it. It's so irritating." She sighed. "I just can't believe that two bright women like us are so stumped by this."

"Let's try another tack," Pat suggested. "If you thought someone did it, who do you think it would be?"

"You know I'm a processor. I can't just pick one out of my head. I need all the facts. I'm a 'whole picture' kind of thinker."

"And what am I then?" Pat asked.

"You? You're a leaper," Deb said, punching her friend's arm.

"Well, if I get to pick, I'll take the young kid in sunglasses who stood in the back of the crowd at the cemetery at Joe's funeral. I didn't like the looks of him anyway."

"Be serious, Pat. Do you think it really could be him?"

Pat shrugged. "Who knows? It could be a guy from the CIA, since Joe had a history in covert operations ...No, my best guess is that it's someone who Joe could have exposed or maybe someone who owed Joe lots of money. So I'll pick ... Father Luke."

"Pat!" Deb said, slightly shocked. "Why, for goodness sakes?"

"Don't look so disapproving," Pat said with a laugh. "He had borrowed money. His reputation would be ruined if it came out. And he's neat."

"Neat?" Deb repeated, puzzled.

"The apartment. Remember the crime scene was all picked up? Cups washed and put away. Neat. So who would you choose?"

Deb looked troubled. "I just can't say it aloud. It's like accusing someone. I won't play. Besides, like I was saying, there's something I just can't remember."

"Don't worry about it," Pat said reassuringly. "Maybe it will come to you."

Deb nodded. "Come on; time for coffee. Let's go to my place. I made sourdough bread."

Stooping outside the door, she picked up a seagull's feather from the snow bank. "Boy, this bird is sure off schedule if he's still here now."

Taking her friend by the arm they walked home.

That evening, Deb settled into her easy chair, her feet cozily resting on top of Strider's back. *It is great having a big dog*, she thought. *I can't imagine life without this golden waiting for me when I get home.* She'd been to Joe's apartment again and had searched his computer. Now, curled up under her blanket, she phoned Pat. Pressing the speed dial, she didn't even wait for Pat's usual cheery hello. "Pat, listen, it looks like Joe was pretty paranoid about certain people in town," she said in a rush. "No big surprise there, but he kept detailed logs of surveillance he did on a regular basis of several people. It almost seems like he was acting as if he still worked for the CIA. Most of it seems pretty crazy, but it looks so organized, like he had a motive for keeping tabs on these people."

"Nicely done," Pat said. "So what else did you find?"

"He also kept a huge file of letters he had written to the editor of the *Press* and to the FBI, the army, and the CIA, claiming different kinds of conspiracies going on in town. It was difficult to sort through all of it in such a short time, but one file was titled CIA, with subfiles for addresses and phone numbers and—get this—another one with the names and numbers and extension numbers of two guys. One looks like some big muckety-muck in the army. Now I ask you: would you go to such elaborate lengths to secure detailed information if you were going to call the CIA?"

"Well, what do you think?" Pat asked.

"I think it all sounds like the crazy stuff that Joe always went on about. Nothing really new."

"Did you make copies of his files?"

Deb sighed. "No, it didn't occur to me to bring a disc with me for copying. Besides, it's mostly the stuff we had heard before. I did make hard copies of the CIA stuff, though. Maybe we should try calling it."

"Yeah, right," Pat snorted. "And say what? 'Hello, just checking, did you guys happen to knock off Joe? You know, the crazy guy who used to call you all the time? No? Thanks for being honest with us. Bye.'"

"Sorry, you're right. It's just that I'm frustrated and really don't know where to look next. I feel bad about not being able to find the money for the girls," Deb continued. "Maybe it really was just an accidental death, and he really didn't have any new money."

"Yeah, and why don't you try for world peace and the end to hunger while you're at it?" Pat teased. "Look, we're both tired. Let's not say anything to the sisters—I'm not quite ready to give up yet."

"Well, I *would* like to check a few things, like his bank statements, and we should check on that piece of paper you found," Deb said hopefully. "And I'll ask Marc about the drug. Otherwise, you're right. Let's give it at least until tomorrow."

Little did they know that by "tomorrow," the thought foremost in their minds wouldn't be trying to find Joe's money but saving his apartment building.

Chapter Fourteen

Marc and Deb awakened to the sound of sirens screaming through early morning hours. Deb thought at first that it was part of her dream, and then she heard Marc get up with a grunt of annoyance. "It's two in the morning," he grumbled. "What's going on?"

Absently, she thought it must be very cold, as the wind seemed to be blowing right through the panes of glass on their old windows. *Someday we're going to replace all these windows*, she promised herself as she pulled the comforter up close to her ears. Just as she started to drift off again, Marc spoke to her.

"Deb, those sirens are really close—might be one of our neighbors. Sure sounds close enough."

Deb opened one eye and saw Marc pull on jeans and a sweater. *That husband of mine*, she thought grumpily. *Any good storm or disaster and he wants to see it up close. Just like when the northern lights come out, everyone wants to come outside to see a fire, as if it's some natural phenomenon.*

"Come on, Deb, let's go see," he persisted.

Groaning, she tumbled out of bed and pulled on her heaviest sweater and jeans right over her pj's. Grabbing all her winter gear, she ran out the door to find Marc—and was immediately engulfed in smoke so thick it was hard to see anything. As it cleared slightly, she thought it looked like the post office was on fire. Emergency vehicles lined the street. She made her way down the street, pushing past all the neighbors who also had come out, until she found Marc.

When they finally got past the fire engines and police cars—some of them, she noticed, from nearby Washburn—she saw what was on fire: Joe's apartment building. The flames were already leaping high into the air, and she feared for the safety of the surrounding building—her favorite little bakery, or even, God forbid, the Black Cat. The water that had been sprayed hung in huge icicles, causing the eerie look of a gigantic birthday cake.

When Pat's phone rang at seven in the morning, she already was sitting curled up in her chair, wrapped in her favorite afghan, reading a favorite book. The Christmas lights on the tree were twinkling in front of the still dark window and her tea cup was steaming beside her. She gazed longingly at her book as she picked up the phone so it wouldn't wake Mitchell.

"Hello?'"

"Pat? I knew you would be awake," Deb's voice said excitedly. "Have you turned on the TV or for goodness sake, have you looked down the street?"

Pat stood up and made her way toward the front window. *How could I have missed it?* Even from blocks away, the light of the fire trucks was dazzling. "What happened?"

Deb filled her in on the night's event, and concluded, "It's something I won't forget, that's for sure. I wanted to wake you but it was nearly three in the morning."

"Was anyone hurt? Did the whole building go? Never mind; I'm getting dressed right now," Pat said excitedly into the phone. "I'll meet you at the Black Cat in fifteen minutes."

As Pat and Deb stood outside the Black Cat, coffee in their hands, watching the smoldering building that had housed Joe's apartment,, someone across town was sipping his coffee and thinking about it, too.

Everything about Peter Thomas was compact. He was short, and not an ounce of extra fat clung to his body. He sported the tan of a golfer, with hair a bit longer than most military men. But then he was no ordinary army guy. His dress whites mostly hung neatly in the closet—he spent much of his time away from regulation army, which was just fine by him. His "uniform" these days consisted of jeans and a golf shirt. Gone were the black suit, tie, and dark glasses.

Taking another taste of his coffee, he turned to his partner from the CIA, Andy Ross. "Anything from Ms. Smith?" Peter asked, as he handed Ross the latest printouts on the fire.

"Nope, nothing at all since she left Nevis," the young man answered.

Andy Ross, an eager and earnest young man, was on his first field assignment, and it wasn't what he had expected. He had imagined exotic places and dangerous criminals; instead, it was this cold Midwestern winter and two middle-aged women whose meddling might just get them killed.

"Damn," said Peter—it was the closest thing to swearing that Andy had ever heard him utter. "It's been three days. What is she doing, taking a vacation down there? Nothing from Mexico either?"

"Maybe she's enjoying the sun," Andy suggested, wishing he had been the one assigned to a warm place.

"Damn," Peter said again, stretching out his legs in front of him. Worrying about her wasn't going to make her call in any sooner. Reaching for the phone, he added, "I'd better check in with the office." He did not like having to admit to losing two operatives.

"Bit early for him to be in his office, don't you think? With the time difference and all?" Andy suggested.

"You're right," Peter responded, putting the phone back in its cradle. "I'm getting tired of just sitting here. What do you say we go and get a good cup of coffee? And maybe have a chat with the two meddlers, if they are there."

"You mean ... actually talk to them? Is that smart?"

"Smarter than sitting here on our butts, waiting for calls," the older man answered with authority. "Come on. Don't worry," he added, his eyes twinkling at his young partner. "I'm a trained professional. If I can't talk them out of this silly investigation of theirs, we can always lock them in a closet until it's over." Laughing at Andy's startled face, he picked up his coat and headed for the door.

Back in the Black Cat, the locals were busy speculating

about the building across the street. Although the air was filled with the scent of smoke, it didn't keep the owner from opening or the townies from showing up.

"Deb, could you and your friend take some coffees out to the firemen?" Honore, the owner suggested.

"Sure," Deb responded eagerly. "I'd be glad to do that." She nudged Pat and whispered, "Come on. Maybe we can get some info about how the fire started."

The smoke was still streaming out of the back of the building. The roof had caved in, and as the smoke hit the cold air, it was actually forming icicles in the air. *Quite pretty, in an odd sort of way*, Deb thought. As she and Pat passed out the cups to grateful firemen, they viewed the damage firsthand.

"Strange how the damage focuses on the back, isn't it?" Deb mused to one of the firemen she knew. "Was it from someone's stove or electrical?"

Taking the cup and bagel Pat handed him, the fireman replied, "Electrical? Huh! Only if there were wires in the middle of the living room rug. Oh, and someone poured gas on them."

"It was lit deliberately? Surely not!" Deb shot back.

He glanced around to see where his supervisor was. "It won't be secret for long. Let's face it; I'm no expert, and we are all volunteers, you know, but I am a carpenter, and even I can tell when a rug has been set on fire. No fire in the wall, no burned electrical plugs, no stove left on. But just don't say you heard it from me. And hey, thanks again for the coffee."

"Compliments of the Black Cat," Pat replied.

"Don't get too close," the fireman warned. As he turned, he picked up equipment to put back on the truck. "It burned so hard, there's debris all over the yard."

"Come to see the show?" a voice rang out behind them.

Startled, Pat turned around to see Bill standing right behind her. *How long has he been there?* she wondered. "Oh, it's you," Pat said, smiling. "Are you part of the volunteers?"

"Not me. Bum leg, I'm afraid. But like everyone else, I

was curious to see what had happened. I hope the sisters got everything out that they wanted. Looks like there's nothing left. Well, think I'll get back in. It's just too cold outside for me. Oh, and I just remembered," he turned back to them and said pleasantly, "I've got a new show of caricatures almost ready. I thought you two might like to see them before they go up. Come on over to my studio apartment any time. It's above the beauty shop."

"Sounds good," Pat replied.

Handing out the last cup of coffee, the two women walked across the street and back to the coffeehouse.

"Thanks, girls," Sam called from behind the coffee bar, as they hurried in, shivering from the cold. "Free cup on the house," he added with a smile.

Grabbing the empty cup offered, Pat went to make her selection from the pots set out in a row on the far counter. The Parisian blend smelled heavenly. Putting in the cream first she filled the coffee to the brim. As she turned to say something to Deb, she saw that they had company at their usual table—the two guys she'd noticed at the cemetery, standing apart from the crowd. And one of them, the compact older one, was smiling and waving for them to come join them.

What in the world? Pat thought, and she hurriedly pulled off her cap and ran her fingers through her hat hair, a common winter style in the Midwest. Deb raised her eyebrows in question, and Pat nodded her head and took her cup over to greet the two men.

Suddenly, thoughts of scenes just like this from every old mystery she had ever read raced through her head. Were she and Deb in danger? No, they were surrounded by other customers. Still ... it was as if she could faintly hear an orchestra playing spooky music. *Oh, knock it off*, Pat chided herself, *this is no mystery*. And she sat down in the chair the younger man had pulled up for her.

"Sorry to take your table," the man said without introduction, "but we saw you outside handing out the coffee and just wanted to have a chat."

Pat studied the man intently. "Interesting that you not only knew this was our regular table but you seem to know who we are, too. I know I saw you at the memorial service for Joe Abramov, but I'm pretty new in town, so I don't know who you are."

The men seemed to hesitate momentarily. Then the older one said, "You might say just we're old friends of Joe's, coming to pay our last respects. Joe and I go way back." *That, at least, is true*, he thought. "When we were young, we served in 'Nam together. I'm Peter Thomas, by the way, and this is Andy Ross. Andy has had dealings with Joe more recently."

Pat turned to look at the young man. He was tall and fair and had the appearance of someone who was somewhere between uncomfortable and bored.

"Dealings?" Pat repeated.

"Not dealings, exactly," the man continued hastily. "I just mean they had met through me." Turning to Deb, he said, "I hear you are handling the estate for the family. Did Joe leave a will?"

Deb met his gaze but didn't smile. "Everyone in town knows Joe and that he didn't leave a will. Hardly left anything at all, as far as we have found. Now, of course, it'll be a bit harder, now that his apartment has burned. May I ask your interest in this?"

"Oh, just tying up loose ends. You know how it is. The army likes to take care of its own, and Joe ... well, in his day he was one of our finest," Peter responded proudly.

"You talk about it far in the past," Deb said, "but Joe always talked as if he had connections now, with both the army and the CIA. As a matter of fact, if it isn't too silly of me to contemplate, your young friend here looks like he could be a character right out of a spy novel labeled CIA. And there the two of you were at the funeral service, dressed in black and wearing sunglasses. Really, who is your script writer?"

The young man scowled but his partner laughed outright. "I keep telling him, he's got to change his image. But the young, you know, so idealistic," Peter chided. "Okay, you caught up with us. I thought you had tagged us at the memorial service, but at the time it didn't seem to matter." Leaning closer to them, he said softly, "Now it does. Listen, there are things that you just don't know, and frankly, two amateurs should not be involved with it. All I can tell you is this: that as crazy as Joe may have seemed most of the time, he was a genius, and recently, he had been reconnected with our two services. He wasn't in any danger—or so we thought—and the opportunity gave him cash he needed to make a life for his sisters and friends. A 'win-win' you might say. But now he's dead, and I want the two of you to promise me you will stop messing around in this. It's dangerous," he said sternly.

"Next you'll be telling us it's a matter of national security," Deb said with a nervous smile.

"Listen, lady," the young man said, looking intensely into Deb's face. "It just might be. So quit farting around with this, and just mind your own business."

"Quite a potty mouth this young partner of yours has," Pat said to Peter, straightening herself up.

Face reddening and sighing, the older man leaned back once more and took a sip of his coffee. "First job. He still thinks he's a tough guy," Peter offered apologetically. Sending a warning glance in the young man's direction, he continued. "Truth is, this may well be dangerous. We don't know yet why Joe was killed or by whom. So for your own good, please let this one go. Help the sisters all you can, but leave the murder investigation to us," he advised. He stood and pulled on his coat, then handed a card to Deb. "Here is my cell phone number. Promise to stay out of this, and I will help you to recover some of the money Joe stashed if I can." He buttoned his coat and motioned for his partner to accompany him. "If you find out anything from the family, call me."

Pat and Deb probably would have done just as he asked—except that just before walking out the door, Andy Ross put on his sun glasses, turned, and sneered, "This is no job for two old ladies who fancy themselves detectives. Consider this your warning."

"I mean, really!" Pat said indignantly, turning to Deb and grabbing a cookie. "I can take him saying we're playing at being detectives, but *old*? I, for one, am *not* giving up until this is solved."

"Well, he did call us 'ladies,'" Deb mused, looking at the card. "But the truth is, we don't know what kind of situation they were in with Joe or if that had anything to do with Joe's death. More important, did you notice the older one referred to it as a *murder* investigation?"

Pat's mouth dropped open. "Hey ... you're right ... Well, I'd better get over to Gabriele's cookie and candy store. I really haven't bought any presents yet for Christmas and I thought it might be good to just go and buy everyone some of their wonderfully delicious homemade chocolates? What do you think?"

"I think it's fine as long as they're all tightly wrapped so that you won't be tempted," Deb replied.

"Well, if I'm going to give in to temptation, it might as well be to the best candy in the north."

Pat smiled at her best friend. "So what's on your agenda for today?"

"I thought that was my question," Deb answered. Putting on her coat, she added, "I'm meeting the sisters at the bank in ten minutes to go over accounts. Whether or not we stay involved with solving their brother's death, I'm still their attorney. We can talk later about what to do next. In the meantime, why don't you try to find out if these two guys really are from the army and CIA?"

Choking on her coffee, Pat sputtered, "How in the world am I supposed to do that?"

Deb shrugged. "Don't ask me. I'm just a small-town attorney. You're the one who reads all the mysteries."

There was silence—an uncomfortable silence that seeped through Detective LeSeur's sparse office, making it colder than the northern Wisconsin winter outside. Leaning back in his old-fashioned chair, he waited. LeSeur was not about to make the other two men comfortable. Why should he? There was a poisoned man, no real suspects, a burned-down crime scene, and now, two "pros" who thought they were God's gift to his investigation. He waited a little longer and then said, "Come on in and sit down." He waved at the chairs. "Don't suppose you've got anything to share, seeing as how you are here to cooperate."

Andy, the younger man scowled, but Peter, the older one, smiled and asked, "Got any coffee?" When none was forthcoming, he continued, "No, nothing concrete, sir, but we're working on it. We have an operative out in the field."

"An operative, huh?" LeSeur said with a sneer. "Let's hear all about it—unless you think us country folk are just too stupid to understand."

"How about you share first?" Andy broke in.

"Give it a rest, Andy," his partner cautioned. He turned his attention to LeSeur.

"Here's the deal. Although I can't tell you everything—national security and all that—there are some things I can say. We're here because Joe was a crazy coot but a damn smart one—he did some jobs for us at one time that involved banking and codes. Vietnam was his heyday, but he did a few jobs for us involving Cuba and China. We're checking now to see if he kept his connections there and they killed him, or if he knew too much about someone in our own operation and was taken out because of that. Frankly, I don't think it happened from our end, but we're checking."

"Well, that's as clear as mud," LeSeur retorted. "You sure about that noninvolvement from your end?"

"Not as sure as we would like to be. But I have a personal interest, too. A long time ago, lifetimes ago, Joe was my friend," he admitted.

"Sally, could you bring us in some coffees?" LeSeur yelled to the outer room. Turning back to the agents, LeSeur continued, "What have you deduced?"

Peter settled into his chair and stretched his legs out in front of him. "Joe was having a late coffee at the Black Cat at 8:30 on the night he was killed. We know that based on information from the barista and from a guy named Stan. We know he usually went walking at night, and we assume this night was no exception."

"Why do you say that?"

"Because the elderly lady downstairs remembers his coming home, as usual. She doesn't know if he was alone, but the time is close because she was watching Jon Stewart on TV, and it was loud. This is interesting, though. She thought she heard Joe going back out about eleven that same night."

"Why interesting?" LeSeur asked.

"Because the county coroner, Ruth Epstein, says he was dead by eleven."

"Maybe our killer came up for a late night drink," LeSeur suggested.

Peter nodded. "Probably. But if so, the cups or glasses were washed and put away. Tidy murderer, don't you think? Cool as a cucumber, washing up with a dead guy in the room. It was supposed to look like he died of natural causes. He looked like he'd fallen asleep in his chair. The killer may have counted on his not being found for several days. That would help to mask the crime."

"Any suspects at all?" LeSeur asked.

They paused as Salvadore came in with a tray of coffees and cookies.

"How about those two busybodies?" Andy asked, while reaching for a cup from the tray.

LeSeur looked disgustedly at him.

"What?" he mumbled through a cookie.

"Deb Linberg is a respected attorney who has lived in this town for a dozen years," LeSeur informed him, "and Pat Kerry is a Lutheran minister. They have no motive, and their only connection with the victim is through seeing him at the coffeehouse and helping his sisters."

"What about the money?" Peter asked.

"Now that does get interesting. We haven't been able to account for his lottery winnings so far," answered LeSeur.

"Maybe we can help out on that," Andy interjected. "It seems Joe owned some property in the West Indies, which could account for a chunk but not all of it. Of course, it doesn't account for the amount we've given him in the last twenty years."

Detective LeSeur's eyebrow lifted. "Blood money?"

"No, we just take care of our own."

Chapter Fifteen

PAT SAT CONTENTEDLY AT HER USUAL TABLE AT THE BLACK CAT. SHE LIKED THAT SHE
had a table that was "hers"—hers and Deb's. She took another sip
of the day's roast and looked around the coffeehouse. She realized,
happily, that she actually knew some of the other customers—one or
two whom she might even call friend. The warm sense of belonging
in her new community brought a tear to her eye. She reached
into her pocket for a tissue and felt unfamiliar items—instead of a
Kleenex in her pocket, she realized, she'd stashed the items they
had found at Joe's. She removed them from her pocket and set
everything on the table in front of her: the empty prescription
bottle; matchbooks from the Black Cat, the Great Northern Bank,
and the local feed store (*Joe must have been a smoker*, she thought
ruefully); a keychain from Sarah's outlet decorating store; and the
last item—the odd list.

So little to go on. Concentrate, Pat, she chided herself. *You
should be able to make something out of this.* She picked up the
scrap of paper and read it again.

Paint by number	24	10
Cash in hand	50	25
By design	10	10
Purgatory	28	5

What nice handwriting Joe had, she thought. She tried to

91

remember what idea had come to mind when she first read it. Something from her childhood...

"Hi, whatcha doing?"

Startled by the voice, Pat looked up to see Sarah watching her, even as she seemed hardly able to hold still.

"Hi, Sarah," Pat greeted her, hastily reaching out to put things back in her pocket. But before Pat could grab the keychain, Sarah picked it up.

"Hey," she said, smiling, "this is from my shop. I gave them away when I first opened! I haven't seen one of these for quite a while. The last one I had I gave to—." She stopped abruptly as her gaze went to the scrap of paper. Her eyes widened as she seemed to understand its meaning. "Where did you get this?" she demanded, her voice rising.

"Sit down, Sarah," Pat urged her. "What's the problem?"

Sarah gulped, seeming stricken. "I can't stay. I left the truck running outside, but just answer me, *please*, where did you get this?" She pointed at the paper.

Pat pretended to misunderstand her as she took the keychain out of Sarah's now-trembling hand. "It's from Joe's apartment. Is he the one to whom you gave the last?" Pat was surprised to see Sarah's eyes well with tears. *Sarah doesn't seem the sentimental type*, she thought.

Sarah caught the look in Pat's eyes, and she laughed, shaking her head and pulling a Kleenex from her pocket. "Oh, I know he was a crazy coot, but there was a time in my life when just everything went haywire, and Joe was kind to me."

"Want to tell me about it?" Pat asked, using her best concerned-pastor voice—not that she was faking concern. She liked Sarah and hoped she could help.

Hesitating, Sarah said, "Oh, well. It was one of those times, you know? When you think you've hit bottom, and then the other shoe drops. I had been sick—in the hospital—and my husband had been running the store, and my son was getting into trouble at school. The day I came home from the hospital my loving husband informed me he just couldn't take it anymore and walked out. I thought, what could be worse? The next day I found out. Going into the shop—my first real decorating shop—I found the books in a mess. Bills were stacked everywhere. Orders hadn't been

92

filled for customers, and the rent was due. I started making calls. Contractors were angry, and vendors were refusing service." She wiped the tears from her eyes and looked at Pat. "You sure you want to hear this?"

"Of course," Pat assured her. "Please go on."

Sarah sighed slowly and then continued. "So there I sat, and I just cried and cried ... and then, in walked Joe. He took one look at me and before I could say anything, he walked right back out the door! But two minutes later, he was back with a triple espresso, just the way I like it, and he handed it to me and said, 'Come on, Sarah, it can't be that bad. Tell Joey about it.' And I don't know why, except no one else had asked, so I did." She closed her eyes briefly, as if picturing the scene in her mind. Then she shrugged and smiled at Pat. "Frankly, I felt embarrassed that I had told my personal problems to the town wacko—a guy who wore the same clothes for days. But Joe placed his hand gently on mine, like a child trying to comfort a frightened bird. And he said, 'How much?' So I asked, kind of stupidly, 'How much what?' And Joe shook his head, as if to keep it clear, and said, 'To stay in business. How much do you need to stay in business?'" Sarah's smile broadened at the memory. "Well, I thought I'd just play along with him, so I counted off creditors, vendors, and of course, there were hospital bills. So I said I supposed maybe ten thousand dollars would do it, but that it might as well be ten million. So Joe said, "Ten million, I can't do," and he got up and left. He wasn't gone but a few minutes—I'd just turned back to the pile of messages from unhappy clients when he came back in the door." Sarah leaned forward now and spoke almost in a whisper. "He put an envelope in my hand. 'Here,' he said. 'You need to stay open.' And then just ... left." She pointed to the scrap of paper on the table. "See this line here—'By design'?"

Pat nodded but didn't say anything.

"That's me. The ten stands for ten thousand dollars, and the next ten means I paid back every cent. I don't know where he got it. I never asked. But I swear he saved my life that day." Picking up the keychain, she asked, "Do you mind ... could I have this? To remind me of Joe?"

"Of course," Pat agreed. "That was some story. Thanks for sharing it with me. Do you mind if I share it with Joe's sisters? I'm sure they'd love to hear it."

"No, of course not," Sarah said, rising.

"Before you go," Pat said, putting out a hand to stop her, "would you look at the list again? What do you think the other numbers mean?"

Sarah quickly glanced one more time at the torn paper. "Well, if this one is me, then I suppose the other numbers might be people who owed him money, too. Looks like they still owe him, doesn't it?"

Later that day, Pat was surprised by an insistent ringing of her doorbell. She opened the door and greeted Deb with a hug. "Good to see you," she said sincerely. "Come on in and tell me what's on your mind. You've got that determined set to your chin."

Deb grinned at her friend as she plopped on the couch, coming right to the point. "I'm starting to worry, Pat."

"Not having second thoughts about your marriage, I hope?" bantered Pat, trying to take the frown lines out of Deb's forehead. Married twenty-three years, Deb would never think of living without Marc.

"It's nothing to do with home." Deb shook her head impatiently. "It's this case."

Pat sat down by her friend, her smile fading. "I'm sorry. I was only teasing. Are you having trouble with the Russians?"

Deb shook her head once more and appealed to Pat. "It's not that. Of course, it will take a while to sort all the money stuff out, but I'll get it done. It's ... frankly, Pat, until now, this has seemed like a game to me, and I'm a bit ashamed to admit it, but it's been fun. Now, all of a sudden, it seems real. This is a real murder. Not some fantasy we cooked up. I'm uneasy about it all. Maybe we should just help the sisters as best we can and drop the whole thing."

Pat opened her eyes wide. "Why, for goodness sake?"

"Don't look at me that way. It's not because I'm afraid or anything, but we *know* the people in this town—every one of them. And in the time you've been here, you've gotten to know them too. They aren't suspects, for God's sake; they're people we've had coffee with, invited to our homes. Father Luke even did a blessing

94

on your new home!" she wailed. "This isn't fun anymore."

Pat put her arm around her friend. "I see. You wish it was the CIA who was responsible, or the army, or just about anyone who didn't live in Ashland."

Deb shook her head. "I know it's wrong and that whoever killed poor Joe should be punished, but I can't help feeling that it would be better if ... if we had never known it wasn't an accident or a health problem—if it just hadn't ever been discovered that it was murder. And we're part of the reason they found out. And now everyone is suspicious of each other."

Leaning over and touching her head to Deb's, Pat said, "Oh, you're not the only one who seems to wish that. Your feelings are shared. You can be pretty sure that from Detective LeSeur all the way down our list of suspects that there are others who are feeling the squeeze. Even his poor sisters probably wish it would all go away. They all must be feeling a bit nervous, although Bill Montgomery didn't seem that nervous about it. I'd say he was one who was more interested in the gossip. Remember? He stopped over the other afternoon."

Deb gave a startled look. "He did? Did he say anything? Did he have any theories or ideas who might ...?"

Pat slowly shook her head. "No, just like everyone else we've talked to, he hadn't a clue."

"No, I suppose it would be too much to expect," sighed Deb. "I just ran into Sarah again on the street. She's another one who's upset. I can't explain it, except it was in her voice. Worried—even scared."

"Well, what do you expect?" Pat asked. "She has a money connection that is bound to come out."

"What" Deb looked at her friend wide eyed. "What money?"

Pat proceeded to tell her what she had learned from Sarah.

After listening, Deb continued. "But why would she be so upset? I've got to tell you, Pat—she's scared. Do you think she knows something?"

"Well, I suppose that could be."

"But she's my neighbor? Has been for twelve years. And I can't look at her without thinking that she might be the one," wailed

95

Deb despairingly. "I just wish it would all go away."

"And if it never would be solved—if it would just 'go away,' as you say—do you think we'd all just live happily ever after?"

"Yes," Deb insisted. "I do."

"Pish-posh!" Pat said, walking her friend to the door. "Not for an instant. You'll be at the rectory for a meeting and wonder at the odd taste of the cake. Or you'd be alone with Sarah and see her putting sugar in your tea, and you'll hesitate to take the cup. And you know what? Everyone else would be thinking it, too. All of them. At least, all the innocent ones. It will never be the same again. No, we've come too far. It's all the way now, my girl, whether you like it or not. We're in for the long haul." Patting her on the shoulder, Pat closed the door on her friend, sighed, and said softly, "And it's just beginning, my friend."

Mike Williamson stepped into the dimly lit hallway. Seated on the bench, chatting companionably, were Sarah Martin and Father Luke Grayson. Mike shot them a look of relief mixed with apprehension. He had been irritated to get a call from Detective LeSeur during the busy morning business hours, when he was completely booked to meet with clients, but he had to respond—Detective LeSeur had made it clear that a visit to the station was not optional.

"Just a few questions," LeSeur had said firmly. "This is important, and it can't wait. The sooner you come in, the sooner we can clear this up."

Mike had been stunned that he was *a potential suspect* in the Abramov murder case—the first murder that anyone could remember having occurred in this town.

"We have information that you had a special relationship with the deceased, Joe Abramov," Det. LeSeur had begun. "That your bank benefited greatly over the years from Joe's benevolence. When was the last time you saw Joe?"

Mike flinched and his eyes flashed. "If you are asking me to make a voluntary statement, without my attorney present, you're out of your mind. I know my rights and I'm not talking to you about this. I'm calling my attorney first." With a vigorous nod for emphasis, he was gone, leaving the detective pondering his next move.

In the hallway, Sarah and Father Luke were commiserating about the waste of time it was to be left waiting.

"It's almost Christmas, for heaven's sake," Father Luke complained. "I have sermons to write and a tree to put up and greenery to hang and people to see."

"And God only knows how many more people won't speak to me if they don't get their decorating done before the holidays," Sarah said with a sigh. "Why do you think you were called in, Father? Did you get money from Joe, too?"

Father Luke averted her perceptive and piercing gaze. "I'm afraid to admit it, but the church can't afford to be selective on from whom it receives offerings. It's not like a political campaign, you know." He gazed compassionately at the harried decorator as he recognized by her demeanor that she, too, had been on Joe's payroll.

"I don't need this," Sarah lamented. "I have things to do, people to see, and places to go!"

"Next!" Det. LeSeur called out, as he opened his door and gestured for Sarah to come in.

"Hi, Deb. I was hoping it was you," Pat said, answering her cell phone awkwardly with her left hand as she tried to keep the car straight with her right. "Damn," she muttered as she swerved into the Wal-Mart parking lot, just missing an old pink Caddie driven by a gray-haired lady who could barely be seen over her steering wheel. Pat pulled into an open parking spot and put her car in park, but left the engine on so she could talk while running the heater. "So what's up?" she asked, staring out her frosted window at a man ringing a bell by familiar red kettle. He seemed exceptionally happy in spite of the cold. She watched as many shoppers stopped to drop coins into his kettle.

"Pat, are you listening?" Deb asked.

Abruptly, Pat came back to the voice in her ear. "Oh, sorry," she said. "I got distracted. Say, Deb, have you ever thought of ringing the bell for the Salvation Army?"

"Great minds think alike," Deb responded, "or at least our minds think alike. I signed us up for Thursday night."

"Sounds great," Pat said. "We'll sing." Feeling more in the spirit of the season than she had in a long time, Pat tossed her phone into her purse. Then she turned off the engine, pulled her cap down over her ears, and stepped out of the car.

Funny, she thought, *the Christmas spirit seems to sneak up on me every year. For whatever reason, there is magic in the air.*

Her new winter boots plowed through the slushy piles of snow as she reached into her pocket for a few coins as she approached the man by the red kettle. "This is going to be a wonderful Christmas," she said aloud to no one in particular.

It was an unusual occurrence to have to wait for a table at the Deepwater. Ashland was a town where one didn't need to make restaurant reservations, even on a weekend.

"I'm surprised by this line," said Peter Thomas to the man next in line.

Bill Montgomery smiled at him. "It's Friday night, and it's winter. I guess everyone has the same idea of getting out. Cabin fever is a real disease here, you know."

"Yeah, right. Next they'll call it CF disease and have a prescription drug for it."

"Oh, they already have a drug designed just for it," Bill answered seriously.

"Really? I was just kidding."

"Oh, yes," Bill retorted. "It's called margaritas. Of course, you have to take the prescription regularly, throughout the season."

Peter smiled, hoping he looked amused by Bill's words. Then asked, "Have we met before? I know it sounds trite but—"

"I'm one of the regulars at the Black Cat," Bill explained. "Even if you don't know me, I know who you are. You're investigating Joe Abramov's death, aren't you?"

Peter nodded, "Yes, I am assisting on it," he admitted. "So that's where I must have seen you, at the coffeehouse. Still—"

"You're next," Bill broke in. "Enjoy your dinner."

Turning, Peter saw the waitress waiting for him. "Thanks. And good meeting you." Deep in his own thoughts as he followed the waitress to his table, Peter didn't notice that Bill continued to watch him.

Chapter Sixteen

BACK IN THEIR SMALL ROOM AT THE HARBOR VIEW MOTEL, THE TWO AGENTS GLARED at each other across a table.

"You do realize what you did, don't you?" Peter asked angrily.

"Of course I do. I warned the old biddies off," replied Andy.

"Warned them off? You young fool. You waved a red cape in front of a couple of bulls. And don't ever forget it. Those two, however they look, are not stupid. And they could be dangerous."

"Oh, please, what do you mean by that?" Andy snorted derisively. "They can't possibly figure out what is going on. Hell, even *we* can't figure out Abramov's murder. And what do you mean 'dangerous'? I have never seen two less dangerous people. My mother is more dangerous than they are. What are you afraid they'll do? Start breaking laws by jay-walking and then run amok?"

Sighing heavily, Peter measured his response. "Yes, they are potentially dangerous—they are old enough, smart enough, and bored enough with their lives to find the danger of a murder investigation exciting. They also know everyone in this town. People talk to them. And you, in front of all the townies at the Black Cat, challenged them to solve Abramov's murder—and yes, in case you didn't notice, you confirmed for them that it was murder."

Looking slightly embarrassed, Andy muttered, "Well, I just can't stand here doing nothing anymore." He stood up and began pacing back and forth. "I need to *do* something. There doesn't seem to be any motive for the murder. Maybe it was just a random killing.

It happens."

"Sure and his apartment building burning down was random, too, right?" Peter taunted. "All right, since you're restless, go check with the brother once more, and then find out if Joe left anything with any friends. While you're doing that, I'll get the court order to go into his safe deposit box—that may be our only hope. And try not to challenge anyone else to solve this while you're out, okay?"

Andy left, slamming the door and muttering, "What am I supposed to do? Look in the Yellow Pages under army, covert?"

Pat decided to take a nice long walk—the afternoon was sunny and still, so she made her way to Gabriele's German Cookies & Chocolates. By the time she'd walked the five blocks to the store, however, she was shivering, in spite of wearing three layers of clothing. She was already dreading the walk home as she entered the shop, but the smell of fresh-baked cookies and warm chocolate made her feel the walk would almost be worth it.

Although a bell tinkled over the door as she came in, Pat still called out "Hello!" to get the attention of the two German women who worked in the shop. Pat had just
helped herself to a sample from the counter as Gabriele came out of the back kitchen.

"Hello. May I help you?" she said, wiping a bit of flour from her cheek.
"Oh, yes," Pat said. "I'd like to buy several dozen cookies, but I walked here, and I was wondering if I could leave my purchases and come by later today in my car."

"Of course. I'll just put them in a box over there," Gabriele said, pointing to a corner behind the counter. "And if I'm not here when you come back, you'll know where to find them."

"Thanks," Pat replied, "and thanks for the sample. These truffles are heavenly." She took another bite and continued to nibble as she thought about which cookies to buy, looking. Then she addressed Gabriele casually. "I was just wondering ... do you remember if Joe Abramov ever came in here?"

"Joe? Oh, yes, he used to tease my sister, Heike. What a

character. He would pinch her cheek and say, 'Heike, if you were only Russian, I wouldn't have to send home for a wife.'" Shaking her head, she smiled. "A little crazy, you know, but a good kind. It was like the war had taken a bite out of him—like a bite from a cookie. There just was something missing. But he was kind to us. He used to pick up the broom and sweep our front steps and sidewalk. Of course, I did always give him a truffle or two. It's sad, isn't it? And now I miss a person who I never thought about much when he was alive."

The wind had come up while Pat was in the shop, and she shivered now as she made her way down Main Street and turned on Chapple Avenue. It still amazed her how many people Joe had known and touched in this small town. *Then again,* she thought suspiciously, *Joe probably knew enough about the people that someone here might have done away with him.* Chiding herself for being ridiculous, she picked up the pace, trying to keep her fingers and toes from going numb. The old Catholic church was just ahead, its warm interior beckoning her. If she could just slip inside, Pat decided, she could warm up a bit before walking the rest of the way home. Pulling hard on the huge door, she opened it enough to get inside and then closed it quickly against the cold.

Pat slipped into a back pew, taking a moment to appreciate the lovely old place—it had the feel of sacred that many of the new churches didn't seem to have. The stained-glass windows let the afternoon light in, giving a glow to the space around her. She sighed deeply, relaxing in the quiet and warmth. *Will I ever decide to preach in a place like this again?* she wondered.

Although she wouldn't have admitted it to anyone, even her best friend, she missed the rush of Sunday mornings: the children, the laughter, the prayers, and the music. But she still felt itchy every time she started to think about going another round with a church. *Listen to me,* she thought, shaking her head, *I make it sound like a boxing match.*

"Hello." Pat nearly jumped out of the pew at the sound of the voice that came quietly from behind her. She turned to see a tall, lanky, kindly appearing man approach.

"Oh, I'm sorry," he said. "I didn't mean to startle you. I'm the pastor here; I've seen you with Deb Linberg in the Black Cat. You're Pat, aren't you? I'm Father Luke."

"Hello, Father. I'm afraid you've caught me," Pat replied politely. "I came in to warm up. You have a lovely church here."

Father Luke smiled his acknowledgment. "Would you like to take a tour and have a cup of coffee while you warm up?" he asked hospitably.

"Thank you, I'd like that very much." Pat followed him down the stairs to the kitchen, where he poured her a steaming cup of coffee. Pat wrapped her hands around the cup, warming her fingers. As they walked companionably, the pastor giving her a quick tour of the church building, Pat said, "Father, I'll bet you know just about everyone in town."

"Yes, indeed," Father Luke said, nodding. I've been here twelve years now, and there aren't many I can't say hi to as I pass them on the street."

"You must have known Joe Abramov, then?" Pat asked boldly. "I met him at the Black Cat. It was such a shame, wasn't it, that he died? He knew a lot of people in town too."

Father Luke glanced over at her. "Yes, of course. He wasn't a member here. I don't think Joe belonged to any church, but he would stop in from time to time. He was a troubled man. Yes, indeed."

"Did he ... talk to you?" Pat asked. "About his troubles, I mean?" When he didn't respond, she went on quickly. "I'm a pastor, too, you know. So I know that sometimes people talk to us when they can't talk to their own families. If it isn't breaking the confessional, I just wondered ..."

Father Luke motioned to a pew. ""Here, sit down. First of all, you should know that I would never tell anyone anything from the confessional," he said, looking down his nose at her. Pat tried not to squirm like a third grader in the principal's office. "But I have heard that you and your friend are trying to help the Abramov sisters with this. As Joe is dead, I can give you this: he did come to me many times. He spoke of his past and some of the terrible things he had to do in Vietnam and even afterward. I pray that it gave him comfort to talk it out." He hesitated, as if unsure that he should go on, but then nodded his head, almost imperceptibly. "But when he heard that the parish was having financial problems, so much so that they couldn't pay my whole salary, Joe started putting money in an envelope—a hundred dollars or so each time he came to visit, and he wasn't even a member. He would slip it quietly under the door to my office. One day, the janitor spotted him doing it. But when I asked him about it, he just shrugged. He'd say, 'You helped me a lot, Father, and it's money I won. What better way is there for me to use it?' The truth is, the church is small and getting smaller, and the people are getting older, and we needed the money." Adjusting his plastic collar as if it suddenly had become a little too tight, he got up.

"May I ask how much he gave your church, Father?" Pat inquired quietly as she put on her gloves.

Father Luke shrugged. "How much? Probably about ten thousand dollars. Please remember that I've told you so that Joe's sisters will know where some of his money went. I have told you in confidence."

Turning, he left the room, and Pat opened the door to the winter cold. She could hardly wait to get home to call Deb. As she walked, her thoughts turned to Christmas. *My first Christmas not to be rushing from service to service. Trying to get in visits to all the homebound. Reassuring the choir director. My first year when I can have Christmas with my family, plan a real meal, not pick one up pre-made from Byerly's. What a perfect gift, and it doesn't even need wrapping.*

Deb walked down Main Street toward the bank, passing the post office, city hall, the movie theater, and the J.C. Penney store. Deb smiled at the decorative new Christmas stars being put up on the street lamps by city workers. "Thank you for putting up the Christmas decorations," she said gaily to the workers on ladders, making her way towards her meeting. The two Russian sisters, Anastasia and Helga, were waiting for her in front of bank, and she could see them waving at her from a block away. Together, they walked into the lobby of the stately Romanesque building.

Upon entering, Anastasia said, "This place looks like art museum."

Counter space covered the wall on the left. To the right were several desks set up in the cavernous room and attended by bored-appearing middle-aged women. A glass display case sat in the middle of the lobby, filled with an assortment of children's coin banks.

In the middle of the back wall, an open door—large, oval-shaped, and with an old-fashioned lock covering its surface—revealed the interior of a vault. The vault housed walls of safe deposit boxes from floor to ceiling. The light was on inside, but a gum-chewing woman a large desk sat at less than rapt attention at the entrance.

Deb approached an auburn-haired woman at the second desk on the right.

"Hello. We have an appointment to meet with Mr. Williamson. He's expecting us."

She stood up and motioned for them to follow. This way," she said, her voice flat and disinterested.

The women gazed around the masculine-appointed room that was Mike Williamson's office; it was filled with leather, mahogany, and family photos. They settled into overstuffed chairs when the auburn-haired woman said, "You can sit," just before leaving them to go back to her desk.

Shortly thereafter, Mike Williamson entered with an air of artificial cheerfulness.
"Ladies, to what do I owe the pleasure of this visit?"

Deb opened her black canvas briefcase and pulled out the Letters of Personal Representative. "We've come to begin the process of preparing the inventory for Joe's estate. We need to know just how much Joe has on deposit with your bank and to find out what is in his safe deposit box."

Mike glanced uneasily around the room at each of the women before answering.
"I'm afraid I don't have that information available for you today. Joe's affairs are a little complicated. It may take us some time to get everything put together for you." Nervously, he pulled at his collar.

Deb pursed her lips. *Give me a break*, she thought. *This is the twenty-first century, the age of computerized records. It's not like the accounts have to be transcribed off of papyrus.* She looked Williamson in the eye to let him know that she wasn't being fooled. In a firm, calm voice, she answered, "You are legally required to release that information to the personal representative in a reasonable fashion, and we need that information today. We can wait while you locate it, if you wish."

Williamson exited the room in a huff, his face reddening. He returned about ten minutes later, carrying a pile of loose-leaf papers. He set them down on the desk in front of the women. Deb glanced at the first page—the total balance on the accounts was $102,000.53. Anastasia and Helga looked at her expectantly, waiting for her to interpret the papers for them. She smiled broadly at the women. "There looks to be about one hundred thousand dollars."

The sisters exchanged looks of shock.

Deb turned to Williamson again. "We'd like to see the safe deposit box now."

Williamson led them past the bored, gum-smacking receptionist and into the small confines of the vault. With five people crammed inside, there was little room to turn around. The air was close and smelled of greasy French fries. Deb handed Mike the key, and he retrieved its mate from the envelope file.

The Russian women looked around in awe. Helga breathed heavily as drops of perspiration formed on her forehead and her skin turned ashen.

"Are you okay?" Deb asked solicitously.

She nodded, wiping her brow. "I vill be fine. The air in here … it is varm."

Mike removed the box from the wall and set it on the side counter. After Mike left the room, Deb opened the box and peered inside. She pulled out several small, tattered pieces of orange-colored paper with handwritten scrawls and several full-sized sheets of white typing paper.

Written at the top of the first small sheet was "CODES"; on the reverse side was written "CIA." The rest of the paper had eight-digit numbers written below.

On the second paper were the handwritten words "Andy Ross" and "Peter Thomas." Each name was followed by a phone number and another eight-digit code.

The large typing paper contained what appeared to be a five-page, typewritten diatribe against the U.S. government, signed at the bottom by Joe. At the bottom of the pile of papers, Deb spotted three IOU's written to Joe: one for $10,000 signed by

107

designer Sarah Martin; one for $50,000 from Charlie Williamson, Mike's father, on behalf of Great Northern Bank; and one for $ 24,000 from Bill Montgomery, the artist.

Deb reached into the back of the box and pulled out a faded black--and-white photo of four children. Two boys, about eight years old and similar in appearance, grinned at the camera with identical smiles, each with an arm around a beautiful younger blonde girl.

She showed the photo to Anastasia. Anastasia smiled wistfully. "That is Joe and Jacob, Helga, and I," she said thoughtfully. "Back in old country."

The last object remaining in the box was a dirty orange feather.

Helga smiled when she saw the feather. "Oh!! Joe's lucky feather! He used to take that with him everywhere. I had no idea he still kept it."

Deb stuffed the papers into the pocket of her briefcase, barely able to contain her excitement, then closed and locked the safe deposit box. She handed the box to Mike Williamson to return to its place in the vault, said "Follow me, ladies," and led the way out of the bank, leaving behind a very nervous banker.

Pat sat at her dining room table with a cup of hot tea and her cordless phone. She took out the slip of paper on which she had written the number she had gotten from Joe's apartment. She'd only dialed the first couple numbers when she stopped and put down the receiver. *This calls for coffee in hand*, she thought. She went into her sunny kitchen, put Sisters Blend in her French press, and set water to boil in the tea kettle. Five minutes later, having exchanged her tea for coffee, she dialed the number again.

A crisp voice on the second ring. "Hello? May I help you?"

Shouldn't they answer with U.S. government or even CIA? Pat thought, wondering if she had the right number. But she forged on. "Hello I was wondering if you could help me. I'd like to talk to someone in charge there at the CIA." She cringed inwardly—even to herself, her words sounded inept. Still, she pressed on. "You see, my friend and I have been helping out a family in Ashland, Wisconsin, after the death of their brother, and you have ... an agent—at least, I think you'd call him that. Anyway, you have someone here working a case—at least, he says he is—so I was hoping you could confirm that he's ... one of yours."

The woman on the other end chuckled softly. "Is this Pat?" she asked. Not hearing a negative response, she continued. "Pat, may I ask how you got this number?"

"We found it in Joe Abramov's apartment when we were helping his sisters——" Startled, she stopped suddenly. "How ... how did you know my name?"

"One, because I have caller ID, and two, because Peter Thomas has mentioned you and your friend Deb once or twice." Still chuckling, she added, "But let me transfer you to the boss. I'm sure he would *love* to talk with you."

There was a soft click as Pat was put on hold and then almost immediately the line was picked up, followed by a booming male voice. "Well, well! You are enterprising aren't you, Mrs. Kerry. Or should I call you Reverend?"

"Pat will do. Thank you for taking my call. Can you tell me your name?" There was silence on the other end. Unperturbed, Pat continued. "So I can assume that Peter Thomas and his young sidekick are legit?"

"Yes, you can," the voice replied. Although technically speaking, I suppose in order to know for sure you might have to check up on me, too. You didn't happen to find a number for my superior in your search, did you?" he asked teasingly.

Pat laughed, feeling a little more at ease, which was exactly what the man had intended, she surmised. "No, sir. No, I didn't. But if I could have your full name and rank I could probably call ... who would that be? The president? No, I assume Joe had this number as his contact. I just wanted to check on these two guys." Taking a sip of her coffee, she added, "We feel obligated to help this family."

A serious note crept into the man's voice. "I understand. But please remember that someone in your little picture-book town killed Joe Abramov. And we don't know why. Our agents aren't who you should be worrying about. Remember that."

Yes, sir," Pat replied somberly.

"Oh, and Pat, can I trust you to not hand out this number or put it in your speed dial?"

Smiling, Pat said, "You bet. And thank you for your time and advice." And mischievously she added, "Would you say thank you to your Miss Manypenny, too?"

"I will." He laughed, and said good bye

Chapter Seventeen

When Pat returned to Gabriele's to pick up her purchases, a different woman was standing behind the counter.

"Hi, I'm Pat Kerry," she said, holding out her hand and smiling. "I left my box of goodies behind your counter when I was walking today. Are you Heike?"

Heike nodded, taking Pat's hand and squeezing it warmly. "Yah, my sister said to tell you she put a little treat in it for you."

"Thank her for me, will you?" Pat replied as she picked up the box. "I will do that," Heike said. She shifted on her feet, as if she was unsure she should continue.

"I ... heard you talking with my sister about Joe. He was a good man. Crazy, but good-hearted. Tell his sisters for me. But listen, I don't know what was wrong, but that last month, he wasn't himself. He was happy about the women coming from Russia, yes, and getting his new glass eye. But he was worried, too. I know. My sister says I imagined it, but it's true. And the last time he was here, he looked out the door and then asked if he could go out the back door. If it were anyone else, I would have said no. We have the kitchen back there, you know, and we have to be careful. But it was Joe, and almost before I nodded my head, out the back way he went. I didn't even get to give him a cookie that day."

"Did anyone come in right after that?" Pat asked. "Could he have been avoiding someone?"

"It's the holidays," Heike said shrugging. "A group of four or five came in, looking. I got busy."

Thanking her again, Pat took her box out to the car. *What did Gabriele give me?* she wondered. Getting into the driver's seat, she opened the box—nestled in tissue paper, like small white jewels, were a dozen sugar cookies, each with an almond placed gently into the center and then dusted with white sugar. The neat, hand-scripted note read *"Joe's favorites."*

Pat's eyes teared as she started up the SUV. *He did have friends,* she thought. *He wasn't alone after all.*

Fleetingly, she wondered if anyone would remember her half as much as this town remembered one crazy old war vet.

Shaking off her mood, Pat pulled out on Main. The cookies called for a good cappuccino. Happily, she found a parking spot open right in front of the Black Cat. She went in, taking her cookies with her.

Sitting in the sun by the front window was the CIA agent. *What was his name again?* Searching her memory as she ordered her coffee, Pat cursed her inability to remember names. That was always a challenge for her as a pastor, but more frustrating now when she wanted to approach him. *Honestly, I mentioned his name when I called to check on him,* she chided herself. *Oh, well, I may not remember his name, but I came bearing gifts. How can he refuse me?* She threw down the correct change, picked up her drink and cookies, and approached his table.

"Hello," Pat said, "remember me? I come bearing gifts ... and an apology."

"No need," Peter Thomas responded, smiling and standing to pull out a chair. "Please join me."

"Where's your partner?"

"Oh, you know the young," Peter replied. "He'd rather be any place in the action than here."

"I know what you mean," Pat said sympathetically. "It's the same in my field. They come into ministry thinking they're going to save the world, and then they find out its lots of hard boring work and little gratitude. It's a shock for them, poor dears."

"When did you finally figure out you couldn't save the world?" Peter asked, with a twinkle in his eye.

"Me?" Pat said blithely. "Why, when a young CIA agent called me an old busybody just about two days ago. Here, have a cookie."

Peter laughed and grabbed two. "These are really great," he said, after taking several large bites. "How do you find time to bake?"

Startled, Pat realized he assumed she had made them. Avoiding a direct lie, after all it was close to Christmas, she said piously, "Like them? They were Joe's favorites. Have another. I can always order more."

Helping himself, he started once again to apologize for his young partner.

"Don't think about it," Pat said, waving off his concern. "It's not as if I haven't heard it before. It was the 'old' part that I objected to." She took a cookie, letting it melt in her mouth, then chewing up the crunchy nut. "But I'm warning you, it won't stop us from helping the sisters all we can."

He smiled. "Truce, then."

Deb arrived home in the early twilight. She felt the chill on her cheeks as she gathered all her Christmas shopping purchases from the car. She had to admit that shopping this year had become more of a chore. Unloading everything inside the house, she found Marc's note, reminding her that he'd gone to his monthly sailing meeting and that Eric had ski practice.

Rather than spend the evening alone, Deb took the opportunity to visit Pat. She walked eagerly up the street to the big yellow Victorian and found her friend sitting at the dining room table, addressing hand made Christmas cards.

"I'll put on the tea kettle," Deb offered. As the kettle heated, she thought about Sarah Martin, Mike Williamson, and Father Luke. Her head was awash with crazy thoughts. She could hardly believe that she was actually considering the idea that one of the pillars of Ashland could be responsible for a murder. "Listen, Pat," she said suddenly, "Here's the deal—if Joe was murdered, and my instincts tell me that he was, it seems logical that we have to look at motive. Let's start with Sarah Martin. What would her motive be?"

Pat passed the plate of cookies and sweets that she had arranged artfully on the green deco glass plate. "We know that she has had major money problems in the past. And she always appears to be running away from something. But I wonder about Father Luke. I was talking to him today and there was a ... a sense of mystery in the way he was talking to me about his dealings with

Joe. Almost like he wanted to tell me something but was held back by more than the confidence of the confessional."

"Oh, Pat!" Deb interjected. "Do you really suspect that someone as devout as Father Luke could do such a thing? What could possibly make a man like him stoop to murder?"

"The same thing that causes other priests to do unspeakable things. We are only human, after all," Pat insisted.

"Well, I'm wondering about Mike Williamson," Deb said. "I was shocked to find an IOU in the bank box from his father to Joe for $100,000. That's a lot of money. And he really creeped me out when he didn't want to show us the bank statements. There is definitely something not right there. I would stake my mother's spoon cookies on it."

Pat took a sip of tea and shook her head. "I don't know if it's going to be possible to figure this out by ourselves. I hate to say it, but we just might need to ask for help."

Deb nodded her agreement, although she couldn't shake the nagging thought that they really couldn't leave it alone.

Early the next day, as Pat and Deb were walking to coffee at the Black Cat, Mike Williamson walked briskly past them from across the street.

"Hi, Mike," Pat called out to him. "Are you trying to keep one step ahead of the bill collectors this morning?"

"What makes you think that?" Mike shot back defensively, as he stopped short in his tracks.

"Oh, we've managed to find out lots of secrets in this town in the last few weeks," Deb bragged. "Things just aren't what they seem. You know, Mike, these are not ordinary times. For all I know, *anyone* could be a killer, even someone as respectable as you. After all, we found an IOU in the safety deposit box that we think proves that you owed Joe money."

A flush of deep red began creeping up Mike's neck. "Me? You don't possibly think I had anything to do with poor old Joe's demise!" he said indignantly. "Why on earth would someone in my position want to kill him? You two are as crazy as Joe was."

114

Mike stormed off and as soon as they knew he was out earshot, Deb said softly, "So much for his being a suspect. I don't believe now that he did it."

With a nod, Pat opened the door to the strong aroma of fresh brew from within.

Chapter Eighteen

THE FOLLOWING SATURDAY AT FOUR IN THE AFTERNOON, DEB AND Marc bundled up in their down jackets, mittens, and face masks and trundled down the block toward Main Street for Ashland's 'Garland City Santa Claus Parade'. Pat and Mitchell joined them as they passed their house for the walk down. Eric was playing trombone in the high school marching band that led the parade down Main Street.

The temperature had been dropping steadily during the day and now, at parade time, it was minus twenty degrees, but with a strong wind blowing off the lake, the temperature felt much colder. They arrived at the corner of Main Street and were greeted cheerily by their neighbors and several people that they knew. Rich and Rita, the B&B owners were there and Jason and Natalie, the cute young newlyweds. Deb gazed enviously at the two couples, who stood snuggled happily together. Several people had brought their dogs. *I wish I had brought Strider. He would love greeting all these people,* she thought. Randy Johnson was there with his daughter, Sunshine. Randy looked like a wooden German Santa all bundled up with his gray beard and ruddy cheeks. Randy was talking with Bill, Randy's fellow artist and kindred spirit from the Black Cat. He greeted them warmly and made room for them to stand on the curb where they could see. Mitchell stomped his feet to keep warm, and Marc pulled out the video camera and capture Eric as he marched past. Deb looked up the street in both directions and noticed that the Christmas decorations were glowing brightly. In the shape of white snowflakes, the white lighted silhouettes glistened and sparkled in the early dusk, lending a cheery aura to the festivities.

Cannons! Within minutes of their arrival at the parade site, the ground shook under their feet as the sound of cannon being shot off down the street echoed up the boulevard. Deb peered expectantly down the street toward the start of the parade, and soon, the procession began: the proud color guard of old soldiers; a police car with its red lights flashing; the mayor in his shiny open-topped red convertible, dressed in muffler and red Santa hat, happily tossing candy and waving. The baton twirlers preceded the band, carrying their white wooden rifles and clad only in their leotards, purple sequined bathing suits, white gloves, and tasseled boots. Deb's heart beat with pride as she spotted Eric and his peers, stepping lively to the strains of "Santa Claus Is Coming to Town." The band looked and sounded good—Deb couldn't imagine playing those cold instruments, even with gloves on.

The display of handmade floats was impressive this year. There was the usual "Jesus is the Reason for the Season" banner that adorned the flatbed truck that carried the live Nativity characters, courtesy of the Baptist church. Then there was a bevy of dancing Rudolphs, representing the Neighborly Bar, replete with antlers and red noses that lit up with blinking red lights. A procession continued with tinsel-clad floats representing every civic organization that had enough ambition to put together an entry: the Girl Scouts, the Elks Club, several churches, the high school football team. The horse-and-buggies brought up the rear, beautifully festooned with turn-of-the-century costumed drivers and sparkly red and green bows on the manes of the horses.

Bill Montgomery, standing in front of Pat and Deb, turned around and smiled at them. Deb introduced Bill to Marc and Mitchell as one of their front-table raging liberals from the Black Cat. Bill shook hands with each man, adding, "You better keep a closer eye on these girls. They seem to think that they know better than everyone else what the real scoop is with people."

Deb was stung by his words, and responded defensively, "That's because we do know more than most. In fact, you'd be surprised to learn just how much we know."

Pat gave her a nudge and rolled her eyes, but Bill didn't appear to notice.

"Say, I have something to show you two," he said. "I have been working on some portraits and would love to hear what you think of them? Do you have a few minutes to come up to my place for a little art exhibition? It's just up the street a few blocks."

Deb could tell that Marc was itching to leave—it was cold and nearly time for dinner. She turned to her husband. "Why don't you and Mitchell go to the Black Cat and get yourself something warm to drink and a bite to eat?" she suggested. "Pat and I can go have a look at Bill's exhibition." She lowered her voice as she said, "This guy has no family and is pretty lonely at this time of year."

Marc smiled gratefully. "Sure, you go have a look. We'll meet you later at the Black Cat."

Mitchell and Marc walked towards the Black Cat with relief, just as Santa and Mrs. Claus appeared, rotund and jolly in their fuzzy red and white overstuffed costumes, a white spotlight shining on them. There they were, perched high on the ladder truck, waving and delighting the throngs of the young in spirit. Deb looked closer. *Could it be? No—how on earth??*

Under the white beard and white wig, she recognized the familiar faces of her dear neighbors, Joel and Ruth Epstein. Ruth, the coroner, was Mrs. Claus! *Now there's a sight you don't see often!* The Epsteins appeared to be happily enjoying the adoring joy surrounding the children's faces. *A Jewish Santa!*

Picking up his cell phone, Peter Thomas let out a sigh of relief as he heard a familiar woman's voice on the other end. "Hello, Colonel?"

"Where the hell have you been?" he barked, his usual calm control broken. "You were supposed to call in days ago. What have you got for me?"

Andy Ross put down the sandwich he was eating. "Is that St. Kitts?"

Shooting him a stern glance to silence him, Peter returned to the phone. "Yes, yes, and what about ...?" He paused, listening again. "Are you quite sure? We need to know for sure. A lot is at stake here." Without looking at his partner, he called over his shoulder,

"Andy, light somewhere, will you? Your pacing is distracting, and this connection isn't good." Listening again to the phone, he visibly relaxed, and then a smile formed as he said, "Good job. If what you say is true, then Abramov's death couldn't have been from our end of things. Poor old Joey must have stepped on someone else's toes. When will you be back in Washington? ... All right, we'll pack up and meet you there." Hanging up the phone, he leaned back in his chair, stretching his arms above his head and smiling at his eager young companion.

"Well?" Andy asked eagerly.

Peter smiled but didn't speak immediately.

"Come on, give! Are you going to tell me or not?" Andy demanded sitting down across from him.

The older man answered, "All's well. Our informant says Joe wasn't dealing information." He motioned to the chair. "He stayed true blue. Our operatives are safe. And so are our codes. I just knew he couldn't sell out. So any secrets Joe had—and believe me, there are things about the Bay of Pigs ..." He shook his head, as if to clear his thoughts. "Anyway, he took any secrets with him to his grave."

"But what about the property on St. Kitts? And the bank accounts?" persisted Andy.

Peter stood up and placed his suitcase on the bed. "Joe may have been unlucky in love and unlucky in war, but I guess his luck had to come out somewhere. Believe it or not, not only have we been paying him dearly for information, but in a sense, he did win another lottery. It's called buying Microsoft before it split."

"But who killed him?"

"I haven't the foggiest. Maybe you should ask 'the girls.'" Seeing his young partner frown, he added, "Anyway, it's not our concern. Let's pack up and stop in at the Black Cat for one last cup. I swear that Blue Mountain coffee is bad to the very last drop."

Down at the desk, the young man on duty looked at them speculatively. "Back to Washington, is it, folks?" he asked. "You have a nice trip, you hear? And come back when the smelt are running."

Loading their gear into the black rental car, Andy turned to his partner. "You go have your coffee, old man," he said with a grin. . "I'm heading down to the Deepwater Bar for a man's drink to celebrate."

Watching him hurry through the cold, Peter stamped the snow off his feet and headed toward a hot cup and a warm bagel at the Black Cat. *I'm going to sure miss this quaint little place*, he thought, pulling the collar of his black coat closer, and momentarily reveling in memories of the people he had met in Ashland.

The coffeehouse was crowded with holiday shoppers and college students taking a break from final exams. Steam rose from scarves and mittens placed on radiators, and the scent inside was a combination of great coffee, homemade soup, and steamy wool. All the tables were filled, but Peter recognized two men sitting in the corner. Taking his cup and bagel, he went over to introduce himself.

"Hello, my name is Peter Thomas. Do you mind if I join you? There aren't any empty tables left."

"Everyone's got cabin fever," the stockier man replied smiling. "Sure, join us. I'm Mitchell Kerry. This is Marc Linberg. But I'm sure you know who we are." Waggling his eyebrows, he whispered dramatically, "Our wives have informed us that you are Big Brother, watching us all." Laughing, the men shook hands.

"Your wives will be relieved to know I won't be spying much longer," Peter said, taking a sip of his coffee. "My partner and I are leaving town today."

"Did the girls frighten you into leaving?" Marc joked.

"No, our involvement is no longer needed. But they are two determined ladies."

The two husbands glanced at each other in amusement.

"Let's just say that when the two of them make up their minds about doing something, we've learned just to get out of the way," Marc said.

"Better for our health," Mitchell inserted.

Peter smiled, but his tone became serious. "There is a killer out there somewhere, and if I were you, I'd watch your wives a bit. Well, enough said. I am officially off the case."

"Don't worry, they might not realize the danger, but we do."

Peter nodded his acknowledgment. "So ... where are they today?" he asked conversationally.

"As a matter of fact, they just decided to go look at some artist friend's work," Marc said. "I hope I'm not going to get some god-awful oil for my office this Christmas!"

Chapter Nineteen

THE TWO WOMEN MADE THEIR WAY UP THE STREET WITH BILL, TOWARD THE CRUMBLING two-story brownstone that housed the Video to Go store and the Stylin' Up North beauty shop. The doorway to the stairway was located between the two businesses. As they started up the dark stairs, they could hear the muffled strains of "Grandma Got Run over by a Reindeer." The pungent scent of permanent hair rinses from the beauty shop lingered in Deb's nostrils, and she heard Pat's quiet sigh and deep breathing on the stairs behind her. "We'd better get in shape, sister," Deb said, with a look of encouragement on her face. "We're going to be biking in the summer."

They passed along a dark, checkerboard-tiled hallway with a series of numbered doorways on each side until they reached number 204. Bill held the door for them as they entered a small, cluttered, dimly lit foyer. The apartment was sparsely furnished but neat, in shabby Goodwill style, and had the stale odor of maple syrup and cigarettes. There was a wooden coat tree by the door, on which they tossed their coats. Several new canvasses leaned against the foyer wall, along with open canvas bags with protruding paints tubes, and jars of turpentine with brushes still in them. A new easel stood in the middle of the small living room.

On the walls were several small, neatly framed oil paintings of war scenes. Based on the clothing worn by the soldiers, she guessed the paintings depicted the Vietnam War. One, in particular, caught her eye—it showed a group of six handsome, smiling young men in green camouflage with their arms around each other.

Bill seemed to follow Deb's gaze. "That's my platoon from 'Nam. After I got back, I had to paint them."

Deb took a closer look, attracted by the sight of what appeared to be an orange feather tucked into the pocket of one of the men. What did that feather remind her of? Of course! The feather! It looked just like the one in Joe's safe deposit at the bank!

Deb looked closely at the face of the soldier and recognized the eyes of a youthful Joe. Suppressing any visible reaction and willing her body not to tense up, she whispered to Pat, "The guy with the feather in his pocket is Joe! They were in 'Nam together!" Pat returned Deb's anxious look with a puzzled one of her own. Before she could respond, they both heard the sound of the lock turning in the door behind them and saw Bill put the key in his trouser pocket.

He smiled thinly. "This is the only way to keep the door closed. I've been meaning to get a locksmith in, but I just haven't got to it. Otherwise, it sometimes blows open, and in this weather, it takes an hour to get it warm in here again."

They women blithely accepted his explanation, unaware that Bill had just locked the only exit from his apartment.

Deb noticed a group of several matted portraits stacked neatly against the wall on the right. The paintings were crudely done and appeared bizarre at first glance, almost Picasso-like in their grotesqueness. "Are these for sale?" she asked as she began sorting through them, hoping to buy one for Marc.

"Of course," Bill answered. "Anything in particular you like? How about those caricatures?" He pointed to work that hung randomly on the far wall. There were several full-body portrayals, some funny and some almost cruel drawings of people in town. There was one that Deb recognized as the mayor, adorned with an elaborate jeweled crown and surrounded by people bowing down. He carried a scepter in his right hand and a small child in his left arm.

"Now that's funny!" Deb said, laughing.

Father Luke was also among the caricatures, portrayed with his head in the clouds but with his feet made of clay. *Now, I wonder why he did that.* When she came to the last one, she burst out laughing as recognized that the two people portrayed were her and Pat, made to look as if they were conjoined twins, touching each other's face. Without saying a word, Deb pointed to their faces so that Pat could see.

"Doesn't do us justice," Pat sniped.

Off to the side there was an elaborate painting of Joe, black patch over his left eye, dressed as a pirate, with a chest behind him filled with money.

"What do you think of my drawings?" Bill asked, walking up behind them.

"You're very talented," Pat allowed. "Some seem a bit mean, but some of these are right on."

"Would you like some coffee while you look?" Bill asked. "I may not be able to offer a brew as good as the Black Cat, but I think you'll like it. I have a new blend that's to die for."

Smiling, Pat said, "How thoughtful. We'd love some. Do you have any treats to go with it?"

Whistling, Bill left the room.

"Deb," Pat hissed as soon as Bill was in the kitchen. "Look at these drawings. Would you have ever thought they came out of laughing Bill?"

"I know," Deb said, turning to Pat. "They're ... creepy. I thought I might be able to pick something up for Marc's clinic. But it's as if some person other than Bill drew these. I wonder what Freud would say about these." She turned to look again. "And you know what's even creepier? I think he took down that pile over there in the corner and hung these just for us. Why would he do that?"

Pat shrugged. "He certainly knows the people in this town. Money and eye patch with Joe, and the priest with clay feet? But mostly, they're just plain mean. It's the kind of drawings where you laugh but then it leaves a bad taste in your mouth. Who would have thought?"

Nodding her head, Deb looked at the conjoined twins drawing. "Maybe you just think they're mean because of this one."

Pat put her arm around Deb's shoulder briefly. "I can't think of anyone I would rather be joined to." But as she looked at the portrait, Pat, too, felt it was—as Deb had said—creepy. They were not just conjoined at the hips and waist; they also were touching each other's face. And the look in their eyes ...

"We really aren't that tethered to each other, are we?" Deb

125

asked.

"Well, here we are, fresh from the pot," Bill announced before Pat could respond to Deb's question. "It has a bit of a strong flavor, sort of smoked chicory, but I guarantee if you drink a cup, you may not drink any other kind again." He handed them each a cup and saucer as he noticed the caricature that had held their attention. "Not angry at me for that one, are you?" he pouted.

"No, no," Deb answered, studying it again. "Actually it's rather insightful. But you do know, we have our own lives. I mean, we're *friends*," she emphasized. "Best friends, but not ..." Her face reddened as her words hung in the air.

"Of course," Bill said. And with a slight cough he continued. "And friends are so much closer than lovers, don't you think?"

The hairs on Pat's neck stood up as he gave them his angelic smile once more.

Pat put her cup to her lips but the heat of it and the odd smell made her set it back on the saucer. "Too hot just yet. Don't you just hate it when you burn your mouth on the first swallow?" Setting it on the table, she moved to the drawing of Joe. "It seems you were closer to Joe than I realized. I didn't know you were in the service together."

"Oh, yes. We were in 'Nam together. Speaking of Joe, have you two sleuths found any more earth-shattering clues? I would just love to hear the latest."

Pat narrowed her eyes as she studied Bill. *This is one of Joe's oldest buddies. If we share all we know, maybe he can shed some light on this whole mess. He must want to find the killer as much as we do.* "Well ..." Pat started.

"We were interested, it's true," Deb interrupted breezily as she looked at Joe's caricature. "But the sheriff's office is following things up. And now, with the CIA and the army involved, we would just get in the way."

Pat's eyes opened wide. *What is she saying?*

Not looking at Pat, Deb continued, "We've actually given it up. So I'm afraid we have no new clues for you." She seemed to just notice the cookies Bill had placed on the table. "Did you make these cookies? They look wonderful."

Bill's smile became tight and the corner of one eye seemed to have a slight twitch. "CIA? The army, you say? You've seen them?

Here? In Ashland? Have you actually talked to them?"

Pulling out a chair at the table, Deb sat down and reached for a cookie, then lifted her cup to her lips and took a long drink.

Bill took a gulp of his own and asked, "So what else do you know?"

Pat joined them at the table. "Really, it was a bust," she insisted. "We found some match books, insignificant stuff, nothing with any meaning that we could tell. But really, we just wanted to help the sisters, you know? And I think we did manage that. Deb did, really, not me. It's useful to have a lawyer as a friend. But tell us …" Pat continued, sitting down and leaning forward in her best attentive pastor pose. "Tell us about your time in 'Nam with Joe."

"Oh, yes," Bill said as he sat back, relaxing again. "We really were pirates back then. Young, alive, eager. If you can believe it, I even tried to talk Joe into a black-market deal. Oh, it was small potatoes. Food here, cigarettes there. It would have been so easy. But Joe was too busy doing his secret stuff for the army. This was really such a shame, because we both moved around a lot, and we could have made a killing." He chuckled.
"No pun intended." Taking a sip of his coffee, he hiccupped.

"Really," Pat said, lifting her cup once more. "I know that Joe did some code breaking. Is that what you did, too?"

"Oh, your detective skills are waning," Bill said, waggling a finger at her. "I would have thought you would have guessed. I was a medic. It was actually great for me. I didn't stay in one place too long, and there were periods of time when I wasn't needed and I could work on my art—even though some of my comrades in arms didn't always appreciate my work."

Pat looked down at the cup she was holding. *What if …* she thought, *what if he's the one? He knows about drugs from being a medic … he borrowed money …* Pat put down her cup, grabbed Deb's arm, and pulled her once again towards the drawings. "But where is your self-portrait?" Pat asked, trying to sound calm. "Doesn't every great artist have to do one?"

An annoyed frown crossed his face. "I don't have it up."

"Oh, please, won't you bring it out?" Pat pleaded. *Lord, I sound like some giddy school girl.* "I just so love self-portraits."

Reluctantly, Bill got up and started for the bedroom. "All right."

As he left the room, the two women turned to each other and whispered at the same time: "Don't drink the coffee!"

Still holding on to Deb's sleeve, Pat pushed her face close to her friend's. "I've finally figured it out! It's *him!* It has to be! He had motive, he knew Joe for over thirty years, and he's crazy! How are we going to get out of here?"

"What … …what are you talking about?" Deb asked. "This is crazy. *You're* crazy! We know this guy; this can't be happening! Our husbands are so going to kill us for getting into such a fix. That is, if Bill doesn't get us first." Deb giggled nervously at what she had said.

"Just keep him busy," Pat whispered. "Distract him somehow. I have an idea."

Deb turned toward the sound of footsteps coming into the room. *I can't believe this!* Deb thought frantically, but she smiled at Bill as he brought the canvas in. Her neck felt tense, like it was in a vise. She took a deep breath and began her self-talk, willing calmness into her muscles. *Okay, Deb, stay cool. What was it that Swami Ji said when I asked him what he would do if he was confronted with a terrorist? Radiate love!* Suddenly, Deb had an idea, and glanced first at Bill and then nodded at Pat with a wide-eyed look. Deb smiled at Bill and in her calmest voice said, "Bill, you are very talented, and I think you have really captured the essence of your subjects. And this self-portrait … well, it's just … great."

Bill appeared to accept the flattery as sincere. "You have no idea how much I struggle with my art. There are so many blocks that I face as an artist that I just can't explain."

Pat went back to the table as Deb and Bill were talking. *Thank you, universe, for Deb's great talent to engage people*, she thought; watching as Bill eagerly described the shading in his portrait. She reached for a chocolate-drop cookie, took a large bite of one, and then started coughing as she realized he might also have put something in the cookies. She hastily stashed the rest of the cookie in her pocket. While Deb was busily engaging Bill in more descriptions of his work, Pat quietly switched cups with him. *He wouldn't poison himself*, she reasoned. Taking a sip, Pat's eyes watered. *He put brandy in his!*

"And thank you for your kind words," Bill was saying as he led Deb back to her place at the table. "Well, drink up while the coffee

128

is still hot." Pat took another sip, and he beamed.

"Bill, your cookies are great," Pat said, reaching into her large pocket, "but I just happen to have some sugar cookies with me from Gabriele's. Would you like to try them?" She placed the wrapped cookies on the table and said in her most winsome tone, "Oh, do get another of these lovely antique plates to put them on. Were they your mother's?" Pat smiled and raised her cup to her lips.

"Yes, they were hers." Bill's eyes seemed locked on Pat's mouth as it touched the rim of the cup. "Actually she was a lot like you two. I'll just get that plate so we can finish up here."

"What are you doing?" Deb whispered. "Drinking that coffee and eating that damn cookie? What were you thinking?"

"Well, the cookie was a mistake," Pat admitted sheepishly. "But I switched cups with him while you distracted him over his boring self-portrait. Quick—dump your cup."
Glancing around, she leaned over and poured her drink into a lovely Boston fern.

"I hope it doesn't kill the plant," Deb said with a frown.

"Better it than us," Pat countered while pouring half of her cup into Deb's.

"How's this?" Bill asked, returning to them with another plate.

"Oh, how beautiful," Pat said. She placed the cookies from Gabriele's shop on the plate and tried to continue to engage Bill in conversation. "So your mother reminds you of us? How so?"

Bill's smile tightened. "She was a busybody, frankly. Always in other people's business. She'd say things like, 'The neighbor had somebody over when his wife was at her sisters,' or 'Did you see how the vicar visited Mrs. Jones today?' Sometimes it was quite amusing, but other times … well, I couldn't stand how she knew just everything I did." His eyes focused on Deb's face as she slowly took a sip of coffee.

"My, this is strong," she said involuntarily.

"It gets better," Bill insisted. "Just keep drinking." And then he looked over at Pat, encouraging her to take a sip. "Joe was like that, too, you know," he continued. "Just like my mother." He folded his arms on the table, leaning on them dreamily. "I thought he was my friend. I thought we would always be close. I came here because of

Joe, you know. It's funny, really. I read his name in the paper when he won the lottery the first time, and I thought, what the hell; I think I'll go see my old buddy." He shook his head. "But friendships like the one you two share are hard to find. I should have known better. Things got worse after the black-market incident. He covered for me then, you know, but he was never the same with me again. We even were in rehab together. Post-traumatic stress syndrome is what they called it. And then we went our separate ways. I thought maybe he would have changed after all these years, but no … No, in the end, he was just like my mother, trying to know my business, trying to control me." Bill suddenly sat up straight and his voice became agitated. He lent me money, too. Of course, you know that."

Now he watched them through half-closed lids. "You found them in his safe deposit box, didn't you? The IOU's? I looked everywhere. I needed that money for supplies. For canvas, for paints, for paying places for shows. You have no idea how much it costs to be an artist. It wasn't for me; it was for art." His eyes took on an almost religious fervor.

How fast acting is this stuff? Pat thought, frantic to play her part. *Am I supposed to be getting dizzy, or faint, or throw up?* Slouching down in her chair, pretending to get sleepy, Pat prayed: *Get us out of this one, Lord, and I'll never ask for anything, ever again.* Desperately, she turned to Deb. "Didn't you have something you wanted to show to Bill?"

Deb looked quizzical for only a moment; then she rose from the table and stood in the middle of the living room. "Bill, because you have been so kind to us, I would like to show you a tool that Swami taught me during his stay that will help you have all the energy you want. It's a series of physical yoga postures that anyone can use called Solar Yoga. I'll show you. If you try this in the morning at least six to ten times, you should be set for the day. It's great for artists who work at an easel all day."

Pat looked on incredulously, and Bill appeared captivated as Deb breathed deeply, flexing her clasped arms backwards over her head before bending over to touch the floor in front of her. She felt her legs begin to shake a little as she blushed, and tried to remember the postures in order. She tried not to think about the show she was putting on. *Yoga wasn't made for beluga whales,*

130

she mused. *I don't care what Swami thinks.* Deb did her best to maintain a shred of dignity in her performance and felt more than a little self-conscious.

"Come on, Bill," Deb called to him. "Give it a try."

Drinking down his cup in a final gulp, Bill joined Deb in the living room and started to imitate her poses. Just when Deb was nearly finished with the series of exercises, the part where she was supposed to snap back up to an inclined position, her foot slipped and Deb fell onto her right hand. There she was in all her glory in a most unflattering pose: her massive behind up in the air, a tripod of limbs, and unable to go down and unable to go upright.

Deb heard the muffled sound of laughter behind her reminding her that Pat and Bill were attentively following her every move. Her nervous laughter joined with theirs—and then she found that she was unable to extricate herself.

"Help," she said, "I'm stuck."

Deb heard Pat giggling softly and then what sounded to be a chortle from Bill—but that was followed by a brief silence, followed by the sounds of loud choking and gasping. As she regained control of her body, Deb turned to see that Bill was turning purple and frantically waving his arms in front of his head.

"He's choking!" Deb cried. "Bill! Bill, are you okay?"

Bill shook his head violently from side to side, choking on a cookie. Deb reached around his back and brought her fists together firmly at the base of his chest and pulled upwards forcefully. She felt the weight of Bill collapsing backwards into her arms, even as he let out a long gasp and vomited on the rug.

Pat rushed over to them. "Is he dead?" Pat screamed as Deb lowered his limp body to the floor.

"Pat, be quiet! I have to check his pulse. He has a heart beat, and he's breathing, but he's out cold."

"Let's get out of here," Pat said nervously. "The man tried to poison us. Why are we sticking around?"

"We need to bind him," Deb said, "in case he wakes up. Oh I know, just what Mrs. Pollifax would do."

Pat picked up an antique table lamp and pulled its cord out of the outlet. "I'll tie his hands with this." "Now what?"

Knowing that they had no time to waste, Deb reached into Bill's pocket and grabbed the door key. "I'm going for help," she told

Pat. "You stay here in case he wakes up." She grabbed her coat and then hurriedly unlocked the door before Pat could protest.

Deb ran down the stairs and into the darkness of the early evening. There was only one place she could think of to go: the Black Cat!

Running all the way there, she burst through the door, out of breath, and found Marc and Mitchell sitting over a table of empty dishes, along with Peter Thomas.

"I need help! Quick! Call 911—Pat's still with him" she managed to blurt out.

Without asking for explanation, Mitchell quickly pulled out his cell and called for an ambulance.

"Just send them to the Video to Go store!" Deb shouted over her shoulder as she ran back out the door.

In Bill's apartment, everything suddenly seemed so quiet. With the snow, the traffic and sounds of people going by were muffled. Pat could only hear Bill's quiet breathing. The room looked like an ordinary room, the room of an ordinary, aging, single male. Neat and tidy—even the art supplies were carefully stacked. This was not how she pictured the room of a murderer. Maybe a multiple murderer, by the way he talked about his mother. Pat shivered. She had learned early on in her ministry not to trust appearance. *But Bill!* she thought. *Insane, of course, fooling himself that his art was worth everything. Deb may have not done him a favor by saving his life. No, thank God. That's not my decision to make. Thank God, indeed.* And for the first time in a long time, she really prayed. *Holy life-giver, I know I haven't been talking lately. It's been hard, but now I'm here, if you're listening. And I want to thank you for being with me even when I haven't wanted you there. And for being with us today. But mostly Lord, I want to ask you to take care of Bill. Thanks for listening. Amen.*

Pat sat in the quiet dark of a murderer's room, with the murderer tied and unconscious at her feet. And she smiled at the peace she felt that she hadn't felt for a long time.

Chapter Twenty

It was unusual to see Ruth Epstein sitting in the Black Cat during the day. Pat noticed the coroner as she walked into the coffeehouse to meet Deb, as usual. But there she was, sipping her coffee.

Ruth shivered slightly when she saw Pat—not from the cold air that drifted in through the door with her but at how close her two neighbors had come to lying on her autopsy table. She looked up and smiled at the two women. "Over here!" she called out. "I've been waiting for you. I've already ordered you both a special Christmas coffee—my treat." The barista brought over two steaming cups topped with whipped cream and cinnamon, with a peppermint stick poking out of the cup.

She got up and gave them both a hug, totally unlike her usual reserved self.

Settling in, the two women looked eagerly at Ruth.

"So, did you find out?" Pat asked, taking in the wonderful scent of the coffee.

"That is, if you can tell us," Deb added, raising her cup and taking a sip.

"Yes, Detective LeSeur said I could tell you."

"So come on," Pat begged. "What was in the cup, or did I just imagine it all?"

Ruth smiled at their childlike eagerness. "Believe it or not, you were right on.

Those cups had enough fentanyl in them to take you both into the dark beyond. You are two very lucky women."

133

Deb and Pat glanced at each other over their whipped cream. Deb smiled at her friend, who already had a cream mustache.

"We don't actually think luck had anything to do with it," Pat said.

"Don't start up on that higher power God thing," Ruth protested. "You have brains and luckily, you used them this time."

"I agree," Pat said, taking another sip. "I just believe in the something that gave me the brains in the first place."

"However you view it," Ruth continued, "I'm just glad you're both here sitting talking, rather than in the freezer at the morgue." She smiled again, "And on that happy thought," she said, getting up, "I must get back to work."

"Me, too," said Deb, gulping down her drink. "I have to be in court in ten minutes."

Sitting alone, slowly savoring her drink, Pat said a silent prayer of thanks. Surprisingly, the whole event had left her energized, not depleted. Smiling, she put her feet up on the chair next to her and she called out, "Sam, another round for the house—and make mine a double." This was a very good day.

Chapter Twenty One

"Air Caribbean flight **26**, boarding at gate **2**. Flight number **26**, final boarding at gate 2. Airecaribe, vuelo 26 cargando en puerta dos, vuelo 26, embarque final en puerta dos."

Hurrying, Pat and Deb arrived at their gate.

"Wouldn't you know, it was the second-to-last gate in this wing?" Pat asked.

"Could have been worse. We could have had to load out on the tarmac," Deb said.

They handed the flight attendant their tickets and IDs, and smiled at each other as they found their seats in first class. Pat was almost bursting with excitement. The very thought of her first trip to the West Indies was exciting, and she couldn't do anything but grin. *I must look like a hick from the Midwest on her first trip*, Pat thought. *What the heck, why not enjoy it?*

"Let's order a drink. I'll buy," Pat said, pinching Deb's arm.

"Ouch! Why did you do that?" she asked.

"Just wanted to see if we were dreaming," Pat responded, looking out the window.

"We're up," the man in the next seat said. "And in first class, drinks are on the house."

Pat smiled her thanks at him and then turned to Deb. "Can you believe the Russians sprung for this trip?"

"Yes, and all we had to do was solve a murder and nearly get killed ourselves," Deb teased.

"Oh, pooh. It was intriguing—well, except for the almost

drinking fentanyl in our coffee part. You know, I'm glad everything turned out for the sisters. And to think Joe had actually bought a house on the island of Nevis and put it in their names. The United States must have held just too many bad memories for him."

A good-looking male flight attendant came down the aisle and asked, "Coffee, ladies?"

"What kind of coffee do you serve?" Pat asked.

Leaning down, he smiled. "We serve the best coffee in the world just for you. Blue Mountain coffee from Jamaica. Would you like a cup?"

Pat looked at Deb, and she nodded her head.

"Yes, please, but please don't put anything else in it," she said in her sweetest voice, and Deb let out a hoarse laugh.

The attendant looked confused.

"Just a little inside joke," Pat said. "Forgive me. And do you have any breakfast rolls?"

"Coming right up, ma'am."

Deb sighed and pulled out a *National Geographic*. "When was it," she asked, flipping through the magazine, "that handsome young men started to call us 'ma'am'? I don't think I'll ever get used to it."

Pat nodded, commiserating.

Just a few days ago, Pat and Deb had sat across a beautiful mahogany desk from Peter Thomas ...

By the look of his office, Pat assumed that Peter was more important than they had thought. Two walls were lined with books. Many of them, she noted, were language texts, ancient and modern, and others were on codes. Pat saw a book on the famous Native Americans that were coders in World War II, and her fingers itched to pick it up and read it. With a smile she also noticed a pile of well worn paperbacks—mysteries.

"Thank you for coming in. I'll try not to keep you long. Get your thoughts and ideas on this whole business about Joe Abramov while it's still fresh in your minds." He leaned forward in his chair. "Since Joe's death didn't have to do with the army or the CIA connection, this is not an official investigation. But he was a friend of mine, a buddy. He once saved my life, and I owe it to him to make sure all the loose ends are neatly tied." His face was unreadable. "And I wanted to thank you personally for catching his murderer—not that Detective LeSeur was too far behind you. He had been checking on Montgomery for several days." With a shake of his head, he continued, "And thanks for not getting yourselves poisoned at the same time. We analyzed that coffee in the cup, and it had enough fentanyl in it to kill five people. He really meant business. It's a good thing for him that he vomited right away. "

"You're welcome," Deb replied. "I think I would have preferred that you had been just a little ahead of us on this one. When I think how close I was to lifting that cup ... I understand now that Joe worked with you in 'Nam, doing language and codes, but how did he come into the picture now?"

"Joe had many connections all over the world, including Iran and, of course, Russia. Let's just say that lately we persuaded him to use those connections for his country."

"So the second lottery that his sisters talked about ... you were the lottery."

"Yes, that money came from us." He coughed slightly. "As well as from a few of our friends, who must remain confidential. But know this," he continued. "The money was well spent. Because of Joe and his knowledge, we were able to pick up two main players in the Iraq War. Of course, that's what brought us to Ashland when Joe died. We needed to make sure that there wasn't a leak about him somewhere in our operations. And also, there was some information that he said he had. But that must be lost now. The fire, unfortunately, took care of that. If he had had it on his computer, it was gone. I'm afraid I can't go into much more detail than that. I just wanted to thank you both personally before I call in Andy. He'll probably want to take notes, but unless you object, I'll record this. Don't worry. It's just to give us as much of the picture as possible."

He pushed a button on his phone and the young man came in so quickly that it was clear that Peter had kept him waiting in another room.

"Ladies," he said, nodding as he took a seat, looking like he would rather be in front of a firing squad than in this room now.

"Andy, I know you have something you would like to say

before we start."

Looking even more uncomfortable, he blurted, "I'm s——" He got up and paced a few steps before continuing. "I just can't say I'm sorry. This is ridiculous. Amateurs butting into national security. I'm just glad you didn't get yourselves killed in the process."

"It's your sense of responsibility," Pat said, forgivingly. "You've been highly trained to do a specific job, and we trampled all over it. It won't help to get angry all over again. And I can pretty much guarantee that we won't be doing it to another of your operations."

He sat down and grinned sheepishly.

"Now," Deb said, sitting up a little straighter in her chair, "where do you want us to begin?"

"Maybe with fentanyl?" Pat said.

And they all laughed.

Later, tired but happy to have finished, Andy said, "It was a pleasure meeting you both. Deb, you can tell the sisters that we have found the other accounts Joe had in the Caribbean." He handed Deb a card with numbers on it. "Here are the account numbers and the bank. We have already notified them that they will be contacted, so there shouldn't be a problem."

Turning to Deb, Pat said, "Deb, remember this?" She pulled the empty pill bottle from her pocket. "I meant to give it to you earlier." Turning to Peter, Pat explained, "We had taken it with the files from his apartment. But the funny thing was, this wasn't a real prescription label. See?"

Andy carefully took the bottle. "It just might be ... And you've been carrying this around with you the whole time?" He looked as if he just couldn't believe what he was hearing and seeing. "If this is what I think it is, you two just might have saved five agents who were very much in danger." And without another word, he hurried out the door, taking the bottle with him.

"Microfilm?" Pat asked. "But I only took the bottle to show Marc and find out what was in it."

Peter just smiled at the women and shook his head. "Some of your luck I could use."

Pat was pulled back to the plane by the voice of the steward. "Your coffee, ladies."

And then after their coffee, they fell asleep, and the next thing Pat heard was the captain's voice: "Please fasten your seat belts. We will be arriving on the island of St. Kitt's in five minutes."

Moments later, they landed at a small airport in what seemed like the middle of a rain forest. *Looks like I'll be able to experience getting out on the tarmac after all,* Pat thought, feeling like a seasoned traveler.

Chapter Twenty Two

DEB'S SENSES WERE BEING BOMBARDED. THE BLUE SKY, THE AQUAMARINE OCEAN, THE scent of flowers. The heat on her body. The sound of the waves and laughing children. *Who would have ever thought I would be here in this beautiful place?* she sighed happily.

"Pat, quit daydreaming for once. Here's your fruit drink, although if you went by content, it should be called a rum drink. I asked them to mix them lighter. But ... oh well, we're on vacation," Deb said with bemusement.

Their lighthearted revelry was invaded by the sound of Deb's cell phone ringing loudly. "Honestly, if that thing rings again, I swear I'm going to throw it in the ocean," Deb said, feigning annoyance. "Hello?" she answered. "Oh, hello, Peter! How kind of you to call us." She cupped her hand over the mouthpiece and said to Pat, as if she hadn't heard her answer the phone, "Pat, it's Peter. Peter Thomas." Deb turned her attention back to Peter. "The fruit was in our rooms when we arrived. And the house is so beautiful. The Abramov sisters and their friends got here before us and are already making it their own. Wait; let me see if I can put this on speaker so Pat can hear."

"Just wanted to call and say hello and wish you a great vacation," a tinny voice said from the receiver. "And also, I wanted you to know that the microfilm *was* on the back of the label of the prescription. My guess is that Joe, even in his hardest times, knew he would remember it was there with his pills—and that no one would ever think to look there. He was right. We wouldn't have found it if it wasn't for your incredible instincts. Anyway, our operatives are accounted for and safe."

"Thanks for not saying it was blind luck," Deb called out from her lounge chair. "Although that's about what it was. How are things going for Bill? I know it's crazy, but I hope he's all right. I wouldn't like to think I'd killed someone."

"No, he's just fine. He's safely tucked away in the county jail. After they pumped his stomach out, it was a close call, but don't feel too sorry for him. That large dose of fentanyl was meant for you. Ironically, now that he is being tried for murder, his paintings are finally selling. The collection of caricatures, yours included, are being billed as the 'Black Cat murder sketches' and are being auctioned off at Christie's, which is predicting large amounts. Bizarre."

They were all laughing as they signed off.

"You look happy," said a female voice.

Turning, they saw the five Russian women, all of whom looked quite different from the first time they met them. Their skin glowed from the sun and the worry lines were erased from their faces. As they settled in around them, Deb and Pat listened to stories of Joe and Jacob as young boys.

"In many vays, I think Joe was a *poustinik* for your little town of Ashland," Anastasia said to Deb with a smile and a twinkle in her eye.

"A pooh ... what?" Deb asked.

"A *poustinik*. It comes from a Russian vord 'poustinia,' meaning 'desert.' In the old days, every Russian village had its poustinik—a very special person, who, for a time or for a life's vocation, lived in a poutinia and prayed for the rest of the village."

"Sort of like a town fairy godfather," Deb said, nodding her head at the idea of Joe's being like an invisible benefactor of the town.

"Another example of not judging a book by its cover," Pat added with a laugh. She raised her glass dramatically. "A toast! To Joe."

"Yes, to Joe," Deb added, smiling at Pat over her glass. "And to no more murders."

As they sat together, the others quietly talking about the next day, Pat saw in her mind a closing to their personal adventure that was like the end of every good mystery that she had read:

As the sun set gloriously over the ocean, the seven beautiful women sat smiling and laughing, enjoying each other's company and eager to start new lives and new adventures.

And with a smile, Pat took a sip of her rum punch.

Epilogue

Pat set her suitcase in front of the door to her old Victorian and looked for her key in her bag. It seemed a lifetime ago since she had been home. *Home*, she thought, startled. *This place has become home.* Home—with her things and her husband and her friends. Her watercolors just where she left them. Books unread by her favorite chair. Home. *Funny, to think it could all be just the same, when I feel so different.*

And even though she hadn't given much thought to her ministry or what she would do next, she now understood that somewhere along the way, she had made a decision. *Just wait until I tell Deb*, Pat thought.

Hand on the door knob, she heard a honk. Turning back to the car from which she had just come, she saw Deb leaning out the car window.

"Put the kettle on, will you, Pat? "

"You bet," she replied, smiling as she pushed open the door on her new life.

Deb returned from having tea with Pat. As she walked up the back stairway she marveled again at the novelty of not locking the door. *Such a blessed relief*, she sighed, especially after being in more dangerous areas of the world. The boys were gone, but

Strider ambled into the kitchen and greeted her with wagging tail and rubbed his exuberant body against her with unbridled joy. The kitchen showed signs of life just left. No note, but her best guess was that father and son had gone to a movie together. It felt strange to be home after being so far away, and the weariness from the journey began to creep in. Her clients and their concerns felt far away—so far away that Deb wondered if she had made a decision about her future path. And she especially wondered if her future path would include her best friend, Pat. *Guess I'll have more to talk about at coffee tomorrow*, she marveled. Just then, she heard the car pull up in the driveway and the sound of her favorite boys walking into the house.

WHITE VEGETARIAN CHILI

1 lb. white beans (like Great Northerns)
2 large onions, diced
2 tbsp. ground cumin
1 tbsp. chili powder
1 tsp. poultry seasoning
2 4 oz. cans diced green chilies
1 8oz. can salsa verde (optional)
7 cups "chicken-like" or veggie stock
2 bay leaves
1/2 lb. tomatillos, cleaned and quartered
1 c. fresh cilantro, coarsely chopped
Salt and pepper to taste
2 tbsp. fresh lime juice
1 c. chopped green onions

1. Soak beans overnight or use quick-soak method. (Cover beans by 1" of water. Bring beans and water to a boil for 5 minutes. Turn off heat and cover. Let sit 1 hour, and then proceed.)
2. Pour off soaking water and cover beans with fresh water and bring to full boil.
3. Lower heat and simmer.
4. While beans simmer, in a large soup kettle or Dutch oven, sauté onions using your favorite method. When translucent, add cumin, chili powder, poultry seasoning, green chilies, and salsa verde.
5. Sauté for 5 minutes, adding a little stock, bay leaves, tomatillos and 3/4 c. cilantro. Bring to a boil and simmer uncovered while beans continue to cook. When beans are just tender (1-2 hours) add them to the soup pot and simmer everything together for another 1/2 hour. Season with salt and pepper to taste.
6. Just before serving, add the rest of the cilantro and the lime juice, stir to blend. Ladle into big bowls and top with green onions.

WISCONSIN CHEDDAR BEER CHEESE SOUP

2 cans chicken broth
1/8 lb. butter (not margarine)
1/2 C. flour
1/2 lb. Wisconsin Cheddar cheese
onion, grated
celery, grated
carrots, grated
beer, 1/2 to 1 bottle

Make white sauce from broth, butter and flour. When thickened, add grated vegetables. (Use your own judgment for how many.) Simmer 1/2 hour. Before serving, add cheese and stir. Then add beer very slowly. Stir well and enjoy!

BILL'S TUNA HOTDISH - *GUARANTEED TO MAKE YOUR HEART JUMP*

12 oz. package wide egg noodles
2 tsp. salt
8 oz. sliced fresh mushrooms
1 onion, chopped
2 tbsp. butter
2 c. chopped broccoli (about ½ lb.)
2 cans (6 oz. each) tuna, drained
1 can Campbell's cream of mushroom soup (10-3/4 oz.)
2 ½ cups grated cheddar cheese
1/3 cup milk
1 tbsp. cream
Salt and pepper to taste
1 cup crushed potato chips

1. Preheat oven to 400 degrees F.
2. In a large (6 qt.) oven-proof pan, bring 4 quarts of water to a boil. Add 2 t. of salt. Add noodles. Just before pasta is *al dente* (earliest cooking time minus 2 minutes), add the broccoli and cook for 2 minutes. Drain in a colander and set aside.
3. While the water is heating and pasta cooking, dry sauté the mushrooms in a frying pan on medium high heat. When mushrooms have given up their moisture, remove from heat and set aside.
4. After the pasta has cooked and is draining in a colander, use the pasta pot (the oven proof one) to heat 2 T. of butter. Sauté the onions until translucent. Add the pasta and broccoli mixture back into the pot; add the mushrooms. Mix together. Add the tuna, can of cream of mushroom soup, grated cheese, milk and cream, and mix together. Add salt and pepper to taste.
5. Sprinkle crushed potato chips over the top and cook for 20 minutes at 400 degrees F. in the oven, until the topping has browned.

JOE'S FAVORITE SUGAR COOKIES

1 cup white sugar
1 cup powdered sugar
$^3/_4$ c. Crisco oil
1 cup butter
2 eggs
1 tsp. vanilla
4 cups flour
1 tsp. soda
1 tsp. cream of tartar
$^1/_2$ tsp. salt
$^1/_2$ cup chopped nuts

Cream first 4 ingredients, add eggs and beat well. Add flour that has been sifted with soda, cream of tartar and salt, beating after each addition. (Add vanilla before flour.) Add nuts. Chill overnight. Make into small balls; press down with fork that has been dipped into white sugar. Remember, one nut on top of each cookie. Bake at 350 degrees for 10-12 minutes.

WHITE HOT CHOCOLATE

1 cup white chocolate chips
1 cup heavy cream
4 cups half-and-half
1 tsp. vanilla extract
1/4 tsp. peppermint extract
Vanilla whipped topping, for garnish
Peppermint liqueur, optional
White chocolate liqueur, optional

1. In a medium saucepan over medium heat, combine white chocolate chips and heavy cream. Stir continuously until white chocolate chips have completely melted. Stir in the half-and-half, vanilla extract and peppermint extract. Stir occasionally until heated through.

2. Pour into mugs and top with a dollop of vanilla whipped topping and a candy cane.

(For a tasty adult drink, add desired amounts of peppermint and white chocolate liqueurs.)

A PREVIEW TO *TOO MUCH AT STAKE,*
THE SECOND IN A SERIES OF BEST FRIENDS MYSTERIES

Who will it be? It seemed like forever, this waiting, like being stuck out on the big lake with no wind in your sails. I'll bet I've aged ten years; it's just not fair! It wasn't my fault, if only ...but no use going over it again.

Dusting off the dried mud from his pants and taking out his handkerchief to mop his face, he put his work glove in his back pocket and looked out at the grounds. In spite of the rain, the volunteer crowd wasn't too bad. Like a big sleeping giant, the tent's skeleton was being put in place and the sounds of the metal to metal was like the waking groans of a mystical being. Alive, that's what it was, and dear God how he loved it. Waiting, restless, nervously picking at a spot on his face, he played the game in his mind for the hundredth time. Who would be the one? It hadn't been the very early crew, taking out the big bones with the tractor. He had known it wouldn't be them.

Phil had given him a quizzical look when he said he had strained his back and so wouldn't be helping with the heavy stuff today.

"More like strained your elbow from lifting a few too many last night, seems to me," he snickered.

And it was true. He had been drinking heavier lately.

Who wouldn't be?

He didn't realize he had said it out loud until a volunteer looked his way with a questioning glance. He forced a smile and waved him on. His mind and heart raced as if he were running in the Whistle-Stop Marathon in Ashland.

Why hadn't I moved it? He couldn't even think "he." It was an it. Moved it before the winter, but the snow came so early this year and the skiers were here as soon as the first flakes began to fall. Damn it! Truth be told, he just couldn't make himself go into that barn again. Not with it there, let alone drag it to the car and ... Anyway, it was way in the back.

It would have meant getting around all the piles of stuff.

He shuddered, but not from the rain that was falling. Just from thinking of having to drag the dead weight.

I should have tried anyway. Restlessly, he started pacing in front of the chalet.

Hell, he could even look in that direction.

"This is killing me," he spoke out loud, and then the irony of what he had just said made him laugh nervously. "I'll go crazy'" he mumbled. "No, calm yourself down," he told himself. "You've had six months to prepare for this day. You can do it."

Turning resolutely, he walked quickly into the chalet, almost knocking over Deb as she came out with a cup of coffee.

"Huh, sorry, Deb." He tried to smile, but his thoughts were screaming, *Who will it be? Who will it be?*

Absentmindedly, he picked at the scab on his face. *Think about the great new season we're going to have; think about something else.* But in the back of his mind the question still rose like a bobber to the surface. *Who will it be? Who will find the body first?*

Deb watched him go, her gaze puzzled, and then, turning, she went back to help the others.